THE LURKERS

THE LURKERS

CHARLES BUTLER

USBORNE

To Nathaniel

First published in the UK in 2006 by Usborne Publishing Ltd., Usborne House, 83-85 Saffron Hill, London EC1N 8RT, England. www.usborne.com

Copyright © Charles Butler, 2006.

The right of Charles Butler to be identified as the author of this work has been asserted by him in accordance with the Copyright, Designs and Patents Act, 1988.

Cover photography © Frank Herholdt/Getty Images.

Cover design by Liam Relph.

The name Usborne and the devices ♀ ⊕ are Trade Marks of Usborne Publishing Ltd.

This is a work of fiction. The characters, incidents, and dialogues are products of the author's imagination and are not to be construed as real. Any resemblance to actual events or persons, living or dead, is entirely coincidental.

A CIP catalogue record for this book is available from the British Library.

ISBN 9780746070659   JFMAMJJAS ND/06

Printed in Great Britain.

CHAPTER 1

I may not have much time to write this. The Gates of Memory are shutting all around the town. I've been trying not to think about it, trying not to draw attention to myself, but I have to face the facts. Today, while I still know what the facts are. In a few days I may pick up this notebook and not recognize a word I've written. The Lurkers can do that, you know. I've seen it happen.

And you?

You'll think it's just a story.

So I don't have time to tell you what the weather was like the day I was born, or where we went on holiday last summer (it was Brittany, actually – two wet weeks in Mum's cousin's caravan), or what my favourite breakfast cereal is. You'll pick up what you need to know as we go along. But I want to tell it properly too. I've got to bait this account with a strong telling and hope that somewhere, someone will read it and know it for the truth.

The basics, then. I'm Verity. I'm fourteen years old. I'm smart, kind, and beautiful in a way people don't notice as often as they should. But then some people wouldn't notice if it started raining toffee popcorn. What's happened over the last few months has proved that. There are four of us: me, Mum, Dad and John – and I've always thought we were so normal it hurt. Dad works as a solicitor, Mum teaches in a school for deaf children, I like music, John plays football with his friends and worships at the church of Bristol Rovers FC. We shop at Tesco once a week, prefer chicken to red meat, and take our bottles to be recycled.

Like I said, any more normal and we'd be in a freak show.

All right, that's not quite true. There must be *something* strange about us, or the Lurkers wouldn't have chosen John. The world wouldn't have gone crazy, and I wouldn't be in danger of having my memory wiped. Maybe you can tell me what it is.

Personally, I blame football. I know that sounds harsh. It's not that I object to people kicking a ball about on Saturday afternoons. But what happened to John that day was not a coincidence. I don't believe in coincidences any more. Someone had him in their sights. Someone wanted to slow him down, and that accident was just the thing to do it.

The Saturday it happened I was watching him play. That wasn't my idea. It was the Bristol Schools' under elevens final, and John is a striker for the team at Colston's Primary. Usually he and his friend Rob go along with Dad on match days, but that weekend Dad had the good luck to catch flu. So—

"No problem – you'll walk over with them, won't you, Verity?" said Mum, her mouth half full of biscuit.

"Mum!"

"Come on, love! I've got my book club this afternoon, and you know it's too far for him to go on his own. It won't hurt you to get a few breaths of fresh air either."

"Thanks, Laura, that is kind of you," said Rob's mum to mine over her coffee cup.

I hate that – when Mum volunteers me for something and then *she's* the one who gets thanked! Like I was a lawnmower she was lending out.

I sat and fumed.

"Verity, just take that sourpuss expression off your face. What else did you have planned for this afternoon?"

"Nothing special…" I began.

"There you are then."

"But it's still *my* afternoon. Can't I waste it the way *I* want?"

My mum laughed as if I was only joking. It's a trick she's got, and there's no answer to it. Of course, if I'd been a different kind of person I could have come up with twenty good reasons for not taking John to the match. I'd have remembered a promise to go shopping with Juanita, or do homework with Sally. My afternoon would have bristled with urgent engagements. But, as always, that idea occurred to me just a moment too late.

Verity means "Truth", and sometimes I think I've been cursed by the name. I don't mean people make fun of it – or not just that. For one thing, I can always tell when people are lying. For another – well, it's like a man I read about in a story once. He had a spell put on him, so he could only ever speak the truth. Sounds okay, until you think about it. Imagine: "Dear Aunty, thanks for the jersey. It's a revolting colour and the arms are so long it makes me look like an orang-utan. So kind of you." Things aren't quite that bad with me, but you get the idea. Mouth before brain, time after time. And even when I don't say what I'm thinking out loud, my face blabs. It's really *inconvenient*.

So I ended up taking John and Rob to the match, losing my afternoon, getting pins and needles in the three toes that weren't numb with cold – and, what's more, I was meant to feel *guilty* that I wasn't doing it all with a song and cheery smile. Only parents can be that unreasonable.

John and Rob didn't help. They were fighting with broadswords all the way to the field. John had taken a length of cane from the vegetable patch and was whirling it round his head.

"Beg for mercy, dog!" he demanded, and thrust the point towards Rob's face. "Or I'll be having eyeball kebabs for supper."

"Careful, John!" I said. But it was only for form: I hate having to sound like my mum.

Rob didn't seem too bothered anyway. "Not while I have my trusty mace!" he replied, and clouted John in the ear with his football kit. John staggered dizzily, and fell.

"John, you all right?" said Rob.

"Course." John sprang up and flicked the cane over the fence into the allotments. "Race you to the sports ground."

They ran off laughing. I picked up Rob's abandoned kit resentfully and trudged on after them.

When we got to the football field there was quite a crowd. I hadn't realized so many people enjoyed watching ten year olds play football. I expect most of them had been forced into it one way or another, like me. I bought a cheese pasty and stood on the touchline, deciding whether to eat it. I was hungry, but that pasty was the only thing between my fingers and third-degree frostbite. I didn't know how those boys could stand running up and down the football pitch with nothing but their shirts, shorts and the dirt on their faces to keep the cold out. They shot and shouted and the ball skidded slippily over the half-frozen ground, and the red-faced referee blew his whistle plaintively, like a baby bird abandoned in the nest. No one took much notice, least of all Milo Marsh, the other team captain. I knew Milo from the arcade. He and his mates were always hogging the tank simulator. Milo was a big-boned lad, with a nose bent like a boxer's – except that Milo had never had his nose broken: he was born that way. Back in the Middle Ages, when football was a matter of walloping a pig's bladder from one village post to another and no holds barred, Milo would have been right in his element.

As it was, he passed his time carving notches in the shins of his opponents. John was too quick for him though. He's a good footballer, I have to admit. A neat little jink and John had sent Milo Marsh flicking his boot out in one direction while John dribbled past on the other side. Milo fell smack on his bum. He looked really stupid – and angry too, as John flew down the right wing ahead of him. John turned on his heel and chipped in a perfect cross, then stopped to watch it connect with Mark Abraham's head.

That was John's big mistake. The next moment Milo had shattered into his ankle with a two-footed tackle. John cried out, and under the cry I heard a skin-muffled crack of bone, and under that the plash of the ball billowing the opposition net. No one cheered. They were all hurrying over to John, who was flat on his back and screaming.

The sweaty ref was great. He saw right away that John's leg was broken. He got hold of someone's overcoat and put it over John to keep him warm. I gave my scarf and hat to use as a pillow.

"The ambulance is on its way," said one of the teachers, putting a mobile back into his coat pocket. It all happened really quickly. And all the time Milo was telling everyone how he'd only been going for the ball. He was grabbing people's arms and saying, "He crossed too quick. I couldn't help it. I was already committed. I *had* to."

As if anyone cared how committed Milo Marsh was. No one was really listening, least of all me. But there was something about the way he talked that made me remember afterwards. *I had to?* No one had forced him into making that tackle. What did he mean by that?

I don't want to talk about the rest of that day. I sat with John in the ambulance to A & E. John wailed. He doesn't cry easily but he was crying now: he wasn't even trying to hide it. Then Mum turned up at the hospital with a copy of *The Midwich Cuckoos* poking from her coat pocket. "How was this allowed to happen?" she demanded. She didn't exactly say so, but I know she thought it was my fault somehow. That cheese pasty sat in my stomach like a paperweight. I thought that things couldn't get any worse.

And they didn't – at first. When the doctor came back with the X-ray results she was pleased. A nice clean break, she said. Should heal well. John was home the next day. We were all relieved.

Let's cut to the following Wednesday. Picture John, leg in plaster, lazy as a lord, summoning us (me, mostly) to bring him comics, snacks, the TV remote. Picture him all pale and saintly, blond hair faintly draggled – he hasn't been able to get into a bath or shower since the accident, and he hates shampooing his hair in the washbasin. He'd just as soon not wash at all, to be honest. He has a crutch, but seldom bothers to use it when one of his loving family is in earshot.

Oh yes, John thought he'd got it made with that broken leg. He was right, too. At least, he was right for about four days. After that he began to get restless. My little brother is lazy enough about things like clearing the dishes and putting his dirty clothes in the wash, but sitting still for a week in front of daytime telly was more than even he could manage. He tried turning the crutch into a Mitron Trooper rifle, firing plasma bolts at imaginary Turbo Heroes but, with no one except the dog to obliterate, even pretending to be a character from his favourite TV show soon lost its appeal.

"I want my King Arthur books!" he shouted. "And my Action Men. Now!"

"Yes, Your Majesty. And I hope you drop them on your other foot."

I don't want you to get the wrong idea about John. After all, he is my little brother. It's easy to forget, now that he's all elbows and cheesy feet, but I remember when he was just born, that tight needy clinging of his fist about my little finger, and the milky smell his skin had then. At that age he was *Essence de Cute*, and if you could market it you'd make a fortune. All the same, John is the most irritating boy I know. He's got this way of switching off like a light when he doesn't want to listen. You can shout as loud as you like: "JOHN! There's an elephant doing the cancan in the back garden!" And he'll just carry on reading his book, or picking the chocolate coating off his Jaffa cake, or filling in the endless football charts he papers his wall with.

That's on his OFF days. His ON days are much, much worse. That's when he gets obsessed.

John's clever. I mean really bright. They did an IQ test on him a year or two back and he was more or less off the scale. The teachers were amazed. He doesn't do so well at school, you see. Once he sees round a subject, back and front, he gets bored with it. Like Lego Warriors. Like Fractograms. Like *Turbo Heroes*. Like – you name it. They're all gathering dust at the back of his wardrobe. But while the obsession's on him, nothing else matters. Least of all his older sister.

A couple of weeks before his accident John had got obsessed. This time it was stories about Camelot and King Arthur. Within a few days he'd read all the books in the library on the subject. But his Camelot wasn't the kind with palfreys and wimples and po-faced knights jousting by fords. His was bang up to date. He used his Action Man figures to turn Camelot into a kind of Mission Control, with the king sitting at a large console full of buttons and winking lights, and sending men off on quests (except that John always called them "missions"). "Come in, Galahad! Galahad, are you reading me? There's trouble at Chapel Perilous again. Looks like a carnivorous Slime Dragon!"

"What's Chapel Perilous?" I asked.

"Enemy Headquarters. It's where they've got the Grail stashed. There's a black moat there, and then three Grail Guardians to get past, each more powerful than the last. Blast – where is that Galahad when you need him?"

I suppose he must have known that Chapel Perilous only existed in his head. But what really mattered was that John was at the centre of things. In control.

And on the fifth day after the accident he got bored with it.

"How come *I* never get to fight a dragon?" he grumbled.

"Because you're the king! You're the lynchpin! Without you the whole thing would fall apart!"

"The other knights get all the fun. All I do is hold feasts and wait for somebody in distress to turn up." I really think he was jealous of his own Action Men. That's John all over: when he plays a game, it's *real* to him. Much realer than homework could ever be.

Now, I realize that's just what *they* were waiting for. He was bored, you see. And *understimulated* (that's one of Mum's favourite words). After sitting on that sofa for a few days with nothing to watch but daytime chat shows and stairlift adverts John was running on empty. He needed something to *happen*.

He got his wish, of course.

CHAPTER 2

What made me so suspicious around that time? There was nothing I could put my finger on, nothing obviously out of the ordinary. John hobbled and crutched his way about the house efficiently enough. He began to look a little pasty, I remember, though that was small wonder on an exercise-free diet of crisps and lemonade. You couldn't say he seemed more distracted than normal, but… Let me put it this way. Whenever he was in the room, it was like there was a conversation going on in the background, a conversation the rest of us couldn't hear.

"John!"

He was staring at a book. Not reading, just staring at the cover of one of his King Arthur books. This one showed a shimmering grail that hovered above a pine forest, more like an angel or a UFO than a cup.

"John! Are you still with us?"

He looked up at last, eyes straining to stay open, as if I'd woken him from a five-fathom sleep.

"Did you hear?" I cried. "We've won the lottery! We're all going to live in a chateau in Switzerland and have dozens of servants. Dad's round at the travel agent buying the tickets now."

"Oh, good," said John comfortably.

It was like talking to a sponge. What attention he had to spare he was paying to the Grail Angel. But it was a sleepy kind of attention, not the tail-quivering interest of a few days before.

Okay, maybe that wasn't so odd. I already told you John could switch off when he wanted. But later that day I was taking him his tea on a tray. As I walked through from the kitchen I could hear that the TV was on, as usual. A man was talking. I thought at first it was one of the hospital soaps John liked.

"I'm going to be straight with you," said the man's voice in a firm, doctorly way. "There *is* risk in the procedure, but believe me, it's the only chance I've got. And think of the benefit for you if it works! Now, are you going to give your consent? I can't move without your say-so. You know the rules."

Then, to my surprise, I heard John reply. "But how can I be sure?" he was asking. "How do I know I can trust you?"

"What's going on?" I asked, by way of announcing my arrival.

John jumped. He turned his head quickly – not to

me, but to the telly, which showed not a hospital soap at all, but a spacecraft clipping the Earth's atmosphere like a skimmed stone, away to distant stars.

"Nothing. Just channel hopping," said John. "It's all rubbish, anyway," he sighed.

I always know when John's hiding something. That world-weary tone was a giveaway.

"Were you talking to someone just now?"

"What? Of course not! Who would I be talking to?"

It was true. He didn't have his mobile phone, and apart from me and John the room was quite empty. "If you're up to something, John Forster, don't you think you'd better tell me? You know I'll find out in the end anyway. That's what Verity means: I'm a truth-seeking missile."

"I'm not up to anything!" cried John, in the voice of outraged innocence he uses when lying through his teeth. "Just bored."

I was forced to leave it at that. But that wasn't the last time I overheard John having conversations with invisible people. For a while around that time I wondered if John had resurrected Louis Patooey from his six-year sleep.

Louis Patooey had been John's imaginary friend when he was little. I'm not sure what he looked like – John used to say he was green, with paws and curly hair, which isn't much of a description – but he must have been pretty small, because he always slept in the airing cupboard, and that's tiny. When John first went to nursery school Louis Patooey rode along in his backpack, and John would share his Jaffa cakes with him (Louis Patooey liked the orangey bit, John said). But when John graduated to Colston's Primary, Louis Patooey climbed back into the airing cupboard with a sigh and was never heard from again. I know John was bored, but Louis Patooey couldn't have come back, could he?

John didn't want to talk to *me*, that was clear. But he couldn't hide the fact that he was having bad dreams. His room is next to mine, and he would wake up shouting several times a night.

Like: "I don't want it! Get off!"

Or: "Yuck – the ink's turned to blood!"

Or: "You're a disgrace to the Round Table!"

And always at the end, a word I didn't recognize: "*Galder!*"

There were noises in the house, too. The stair creaked as if someone was prowling softly and furtively about the place. The plates chinked downstairs, and I saw the light in the bathroom flicker on and off sometimes, even when Mum and Dad were both asleep and snoring. And there was a buzzing in my ears, half cicada, half discreet ringtone, that came and went through the night like a ghost. Only it wasn't creepy in a ghostly way, even though I got goose pimples. It was more like, say, static electricity. Like we might be in for a thunderstorm. Which was more or less right, when you think about it.

On Sunday evening we were watching *Antiques Roadshow*. John likes to impress me by knowing the proper names for all the different kinds of furniture: goodness knows where he learns it all. He was sitting in a crinkly sea of sweet wrappers, his hair looking even more unwashed and lank than usual. He didn't move when I sat on the sofa beside him.

"How's the leg?" I said, by way of making conversation.

"Itchy!" he said. He sounded more like himself when he was complaining. "I wish this cast could come off. If I kicked it hard against the wall, do you think maybe it would crack open?"

"No."

"You know, like an egg?"

"Don't be stupid," I said.

"Stupid yourself."

A lot of our conversations go like this. For a while we both sat huffily watching TV. As usual, it was me who made the first move.

"It'll be off anyway in five weeks. You heard what the doctor said. It was a clean break. You were lucky."

"Five weeks is *for ever*!" complained John.

"March the twentieth, actually. Five weeks tomorrow. Your appointment's on the calendar."

John looked at me with a curious expression on his chocolate-covered face. "Tomorrow never comes," he said profoundly.

"You're mistaken," I replied.

"We'll see about that," he said, and flipped the channel again.

I thought no more about it at the time. John's the sort of boy who's always got to have the last word, and luckily I am able to rise above such pettiness. We're a perfect match, Dad says.

But next morning, when I woke with the sunlight slamming into my eyelids like a battering ram, I panicked. What had happened to my alarm? On weekdays I get up at seven, sharp, to feed the dog and lay the breakfast things. It was still winter, and for it to be this light I must be running very late. I winched my eyes open double quick. The clock said 8.45 a.m.

"Mum! Dad!"

I was clattering down the stairs. From my parents' room dim sounds of protest could be heard. Mum groaned like a hydra with a hangover.

Dad had appeared at the bedroom door.

"What is it?" he said, glaring at me with red-rimmed eyes.

"Quarter to nine, that's what it is!"

"So?" he yawned, opening his mouth so wide I could see the wobbly thing at the back of his throat. "It's Sunday, if you hadn't noticed."

"*Sunday?*"

"Sunday," he repeated. The bedroom door closed solidly in my face. I heard him grumbling back across the room to Mum, and Mum grumbling faintly back. "What do you mean, *my* daughter – she's yours too!" were the only words I could make out. Charming. Then everything went very quiet again. Sunday quiet, with only the low-volume hysterics of the cartoon shows coming from the living room below.

Plop!

A bundle of papers had fallen onto the doormat. Fifteen different supplements and colour sections spread slowly across the hall floor like lava. It was Monday morning, and the Sunday papers had just arrived.

By the time I got to the kitchen I wondered if I was going crazy. Yesterday was clear in my mind. Mum listening to *The Archers* omnibus on the radio, Dad playing badminton before traipsing off to the pub at lunchtime, me taking Jump Jet Harry, our Jack Russell terrier, for a walk round the park, then John beating me at Monopoly by the light of MTV half the afternoon. It had been the same as any other Sunday, but it was real enough.

Like I said, by the time I got to the kitchen, I thought I was mad. A moment later I was sure of it.

The fridge door was hanging open and the work counter was a mess, with milk and chocolate powder everywhere. A chocolatey spoon lay on the lino. That wasn't so unusual. I assumed John had hobbled out to get himself a sugar fix. But then I saw it. Floating towards me, a metre from the floor, was a mug of hot chocolate. I found myself backing against the wall as it passed. It was close enough for me to be quite sure: there were no strings, no mirrors, no visible means of support. Only, as it wobbled on its way to the hall, I saw a *shiver* in the light, the size and shape of a short man. Actually, I didn't exactly *see* it. I *felt* it though, down the back of my neck. Then the mug was disappearing past the coat hooks by the front door and turning sharp left (too sharp – a gollop of hot chocolate slopped onto the mat) into the living room.

I wanted to run screaming back to my parents. But I didn't. John was in the living room. I knew he'd freak when he saw that ghostly mug floating in front of Fox Kids. I had to save him.

That's what I tried to tell myself, anyway. The truth is, I think I knew right away that John was behind it all. I got to the living room just in time to see. There was John, leg up on the coffee table, with the remote in his hand. *Mona the Vampire* was on the telly. And kneeling to one side (so as not to block John's view of the screen, perhaps) was a – *thing*. It was handing him the mug.

I must have screamed a bit, because John almost leaped out of his seat, plaster cast and all. His face went red as he looked from the Thing to me and back again. "Morning," said John, desperately trying to sound normal. "Wanna watch? It's almost time for that music programme you like…"

I didn't move from the doorway. "John – what *is* that?"

He seemed amazed I was able to see it. Didn't he know I was Verity, the Truth Hound? I could hear his brain whirring, wondering what story to tell me.

In the end he said quite simply, as if introducing a stranger: "This…is Galder."

The shadowy thing turned to me. Its red eyes blinked. It stood and bowed in a courtly way – a sarcastic way, perhaps. I told myself it wasn't really there. Whatever it was it was all done with holograms, or something.

That mug of hot chocolate was real enough, though.

"Your humble servant," said Galder. It didn't speak out loud, but the voice inside my head was clear – and it was as cold and greasy as yesterday's washing-up water.

"He's a refugee," John explained. Galder nodded plaintively at his side. He crouched low, as if he were used to being kicked hard and often. "I promised to give him shelter. Galder's going to be staying here from now on."

He leaned forward and added, more as a statement than a question: "You won't tell anyone, will you?"

CHAPTER 3

I could see Galder more plainly now: I think he'd chosen to let me. His hair was parted in two sticky waves, and curled a little just at the top of his ears. He was dressed in a baggy grey suit that looked like it had been thrown out by Oxfam. There was a stale, mildewy smell about him. Galder was looking at me, but his eyes kept veering off towards John, as though he was afraid John would disappear if he didn't keep an eye on him.

"A refugee?" I repeated. "Where from? What did he do?"

I spoke rudely. I think that's because I was afraid of him: fear made me angry. What a nerve Galder had, barging in like that!

I knew even then that he was trying to control my response. It was radiating from him like heat from a stove, a feeling that said, "I'm harmless; don't mind me; I'll fit right in; I've the appetite of a sparrow."

"You'll be Master John's big sister, then?" he cringed. "Miss Verity, am I right?"

"I'm Verity," I said coldly. "And who are you? More to the point, what are you doing in our house at nine o'clock on a Monday morning?"

"*Sun*day morning," John put in. "I told you it would be."

"Shut up, you! Mum and Dad are going to hit

the roof when they find out you've been inviting strangers into the house."

Galder winced, as if my voice was edged like a saw. "There's no need for unpleasantness," he said. "I'll go."

"No! I want you to stay, Galder," exclaimed John. "You must."

Galder gave him a smile – or at least, the line where his mouth was bent like a bow, but there was nothing very cheery about it. "I'll be back soon," he assured John. "You'll hardly know I was gone."

And then Galder wasn't there. I saw him smiling at John, and then it was as if someone had blown a Galder-shaped smoke ring, and the outlines of his body thinned and whitened, and in the space of a breath there was no Galder – at least that I could see.

Without Galder to back him up, John seemed to shrink a bit too. He looked a lot less cocky, suddenly. But he put a brave face on it. "It's all right," he said, "there's no need to say anything. I can tell you don't like him."

"*John!*" I shouted – a whispering kind of shout, because if this really was Sunday morning Mr. Stimson next door would bang on the wall if anyone so much as patted the dog before ten. "How long has that sleazy ghost been hanging around?"

"He's not a ghost!"

"Well, *I* could see right through him."

"Shh! Don't talk about Galder like that! He's very sensitive about his appearance."

"*What do you think you're getting into here?*" I shout-whispered.

John sighed. "He tries his best to be real, you know. Anyway, you're the one who's always on about helping refugees."

"Just tell me who he is, John, and stop changing the subject," I whisper-shouted.

"He was a slave," muttered John. "I'd have thought you'd be more sympathetic."

"There aren't any slaves," I said, not entirely certain. "Not these days."

"There are where he comes from," said John. "He's not human, Verity, in case you'd missed that."

"Where does he come from then? Planet Sleazebag?"

"Course not!" protested John.

Then for a moment I imagined something so vividly that I really thought it was happening. I thought that John leaned forward (as far as he could, with his leg in plaster) and tapped his head knowingly: "He lives in *here*, Miss!" Except that it wasn't John talking at all. The voice was his, but it had been smoothed down and curled at the edges, like Galder's sticky hair.

"I'm giving him shelter," was what John actually said.

This was getting beyond a joke. I don't like pulling the big-sister act, but I didn't have much choice. "Right," I said. "That's it. I'm going to go and tell

Mum and Dad about this mate of yours right now."

"No. You can't. *I don't want you to talk about it.*"

"We'll see about that!"

This time I forgot to whisper. Mr. Stimson thumped on the wall so promptly he must have been waiting just the other side with his walking stick poised, but I didn't care. I ran back into the hall, skidding across the slick of Sunday supplements by the front door, and pounded up to Mum and Dad's room.

Dad was already sitting up in bed, reading a book. He almost dropped it when I burst in.

"Where's the fire, Verity? Don't you know it's a day of rest?"

"This is important!"

Dad raised his eyebrows in a sceptical, lawyerish way, and peered at me over the top of his half-moon glasses.

"It's John. He's got a – a –"

"Yes?" drawled my father, still more sceptically. "What has he got?"

"I...don't know exactly. It's not something I've ever seen before..."

I was stumbling, I knew it. I could feel myself going red, as if I were doing something very foolish. But what did you call Galder? A ghost? An alien? A stray?

"He's got...a new friend," I said lamely. "I don't like him."

By this time even Mum was awake again – and she'll normally sleep through a marching band of Mr. Stimsons all beating their sticks in unison. "Whatshee" – *yawn* – "talkin'" – *yawn* – "'bout?"

"I'm not entirely sure as yet, my love. Apparently John's taken up with some new friend Verity disapproves of. Though why that should be so urgent is beyond me."

"It's not just that. This new friend, he...*does* things."

"Did you hear that, my love? He does things. Are you sure, Verity?" My father's stare was getting more sarcastic and lawyerish by the second. "A charge of 'doing things' is not to be made lightly."

It wasn't that I didn't want to tell them about Galder: I was desperate to tell. But every time I opened my mouth it was as if someone had released a trapdoor at the bottom of my mind and let all the words fall out. I stood there gaping like a carp.

"But…but…"

Then I remembered. *I don't want you to talk about it*, John had said.

Of course, it was all his doing.

"Mum!" came John's voice from below. "Can you send Verity down? I really need a bowl of Frosted Shreddies!"

I don't remember much more about that morning. It was like a dream – the kind where you know you're dreaming and can't wake up. Mum and Dad came downstairs a bit later and began picking through the paper, like vultures squabbling over a carcass. They grunted their way through breakfast, then Dad grabbed his badminton racquet and set off for the gym, where he played his mate George from work every Sunday. I remember wondering if George and the staff at the Sports Centre were reliving their Sundays too. Surely Galder's magic couldn't be strong enough to affect the whole town?

Apparently it could. Dad came in a couple of hours later, pink and puffing, having jogged back from the badminton court "On the wings of a famous victory", as he put it. (Dad can get a bit poetical when he's excited.)

"Did everyone seem…all right?" I asked in an exploratory way.

"All right? Even the aerobics class on the far side of the gym was cheering by the end! That last backhand smash…"

John smirked at me across the kitchen table where he was pretending to read his football book. Did I see

Galder's red eyes shining behind John's straggle of unwashed blond hair? Or was John just trying to rile me, as usual?

Through it all I had to keep reminding myself that *I* knew what was true. Maybe I should have been wondering by this time whether I was imagining it, or going quietly crazy after all, but I didn't. I am Verity. I couldn't lie, even to myself. Galder *was* real, and it *was* Monday, or should have been. And I *did* have a jinx stopping me from talking about him to anyone but John.

And John – how did I feel about him? He'd been pretty sneaky, but I could see he'd been jinxed by Galder a bit too. Galder hadn't popped out of any lamp, but there he was, a shabby, Brylcreemed genie, ready to grant him wishes. What better way of passing the time could a lazy, ten-year-old invalid ask for? It was irresistible. My guess is that John thought this was still some kind of game – and a way of getting one over on his big sister, of course. John's always needed me to be impressed, though he'd rather die than admit it.

Besides, getting Galder to make him a hot drink wasn't much of a crime, I supposed. And a three-day weekend – where was the harm in that?

These kindly thoughts lasted until I got to my own bedroom door.

Now, I like my bedroom a lot. It's got a big bay window looking out over the street, and a stripy sofa for lazing on. I like to watch the people going past outside; it's like my own private show. Today, though, something was different. Even on the landing things didn't seem quite normal. Had that photo of Mum as a little girl really been hanging so close to the bathroom door? Hadn't there been three panes of glass, not two, in the skylight? I'm not sure I stopped to think about it at the time (who's sad enough to go round counting window panes?) but looking back, I already knew something was wrong.

I went into my room, and prepared to flop onto

my sofa. But in mid-flop I stumbled and tripped on a rug that hadn't been there before. The next moment I hit my forehead on the opposite wall. Finally I slumped, head spinning, onto an armrest.

What was going on? My wardrobe, which should have had a large spiral-patterned rug in front of it, was standing *on* the rug instead. I remember thinking someone must have been in my room and rearranged the furniture. But it was more than that. Normally there would have been plenty of room for that rug to lie in front of the wardrobe, with half a metre to spare. But now the far end of the rug was right up against the wall, curling against the wainscoting like the hair over the tops of Galder's ears.

I couldn't deny it.

The room had *shrunk*.

"John!" I yelled. "John Christian Forster! Limp up here right now!"

Within a second Mum was at the foot of the stairs, shouting back: "Verity! You can't expect your brother to come trailing after you when he has his leg in plaster."

"It's all right, Mum," said John's voice, sounding sickeningly saintly. "I was going up anyway."

Mum subsided at once. "You mustn't let Verity boss you around like that," she chided him fondly.

Even from Mum, that was a bit rich! Hadn't she noticed John treating me like a servant for the last couple of weeks? Galder couldn't have made her forget that, could he?

But I didn't have time to worry about it. John was clumping up towards me. I noticed that the air behind him was quivering slightly, like the heat haze over a road on a hot day. And John looked like he was walking through that desert heat. His face was strained, his blond hair straggling down his face in snaky coils.

"What's this all about?" he asked wearily.

"What do you think? What have you done to my room?"

"*Your* room?" he said in surprise. "But I –"

I dragged him to the door and turned his head to see. Now I was looking properly it was obvious. The wall between my room and his had moved forward by a metre, tumbling all my things with it, rucking rugs and spilling the earth from my cactus pots. Only the fact that my room's a bit of a mess at the best of times had disguised it.

"Don't tell me this has nothing to do with you," I warned.

John was a little shaken. "It was the Scalextric, you see. I needed the extra space to get up enough speed to loop the loop."

He hurried to his own doorway, and looked greatly relieved when he peered inside. I must have been stupid, but it only then occurred to me that if *my* room was one metre smaller, then *his* must have grown by the same amount. That was the point, I suppose. He'd only been thinking about himself.

"Galder?" said John.

Instantly Galder was standing there on the landing, his servile hands clasping each other.

"Master John?" said Galder oozingly. "You are ill at ease?"

John didn't even seem to notice the way Galder was sucking up to him. He said in his ordinary way: "When I said I wanted enough space for the loop-the-loop, all I meant was—"

"And now you have it, Master John," said Galder with a flourish. And somehow we were all inside John's room, staring around us from the middle of his carpet.

It *was* John's room, but it was transformed. The *Lord of the Rings* duvet cover no longer showed a faded picture of the Battle of Pelennor Fields. It was actually moving, with blades and axes whirring and a chinking chorus of swords and shields. As my eye slid from that to the NASA picture above John's computer desk the sound of battle faded, to be replaced by the *whoosh* of a comet. It flamed from his hologrammatic poster into the room. I ducked before I realized it wasn't real.

There were lots of other changes like that. Some of John's Action Men were on manoeuvres under his bunk bed (you could hear them coughing with the dust down there). The brass St. George-and-the-Dragon bookends at either end of his shelf were struggling to reach each other, too – the knight's horse rearing and the dragon writhing like a worm that's been chopped in half. The room was jiggling with movement and life. Except that none of it was real. I had to believe that. All this movement was Galder's trickery – distractions, lies. The room really did seem to be bigger, though. And I could see what John had meant about the loop-the-loop. His old Scalextric was set out across the floor, but it had grown vast; there was four times as much track, and the cars had turned from matchbox-sized models to sleek growling roadsters. The loop-the-loop was nestling under his Bristol Rovers season wallchart.

"You can see why I needed the space," John explained apologetically.

"Put it back, John." I spoke slowly and clearly. You would never have guessed I was scared silly. "Put – it – back. Now."

"I can't! You don't understand. It doesn't work like that…"

"Of course it does! Just tell your little friend to put everything back the way it was."

John began to answer, but as he opened his mouth his whole expression changed. It didn't change much, perhaps. Just the creases at the corners of his eyes deepened, making him look older. And the mouth was curved at the edges with Galder's insincere quizmaster smile. Galder himself seemed to have vanished.

"The way it was?" John repeated, in a new, slow, musical voice. "But our rooms have always been this way." And he looked at me very hard and stonily as he said it, as if he could crush me with the force of his words.

The words hit me like a belly punch. I shut my eyes, overcome with a horrible nauseous dizziness. "*They've always been this way*," he said again – and it was Galder that spoke, even if he used John's voice to do it. "*Alwaaays…*"

The word slid through the cracks of my mind like oil into a rusty hinge, easing it open.

But I didn't buckle. I am Verity. I see the truth – it's the way I'm made. Instead, I opened my eyes and slapped John hard. He staggered and nearly fell, clutching his face in shock, his cheek pink. "What did you do that for?" he croaked. It was John talking again. I don't think he even knew what had happened. "You're crazy," he said. His eyes were already fillin "Psycho!"

"You're the crazy one! Can't you see that your so-called friend is only out to use you? You've got to get out of this now, John, before it's too late!"

John wiped his eyes. "Galder warned me you'd be like this," he said, and looked at me with a naked dislike I'd never seen on his face. He'd been angry with me before, of course. We argued twenty times a day like brothers and sisters do, but this – this was *hatred*. "Can't stand it, can you?" he said. The whiny snarl matched his expression perfectly. "You can't stand to see me getting a break for once. You've got to come and ruin my good luck."

The utter unfairness of this left me speechless. "I… I haven't ever…"

"You won't even admit it!" he said with contempt. "Well, the tables are turned now. Me and Galder are going to make things go *my* way for a change. And you'd better get used to it, because getting myself a decent-sized room is only the start!"

A door slammed, and somehow I was standing out on the landing again, with his words echoing in my ears.

"You little fool, John Forster," I said to myself. "Can't you see this is about more than getting one over on me? Haven't you stopped to wonder what Galder's up to?"

CHAPTER 4

Here's a strange thing. All this time none of John's friends had called to ask how he was. He'd received a mass Get Well card from his class a couple of days after the accident, but that was an obvious put-up job by the teacher – you could tell by the dutiful way everyone had printed their names in neat school-lesson script. The picture on the front showed John, in football kit and with a ball under his arm, smiling. He'd been pleased enough to get it at the time.

Since then, though, there had been silence. Weird silence. Our house was on the way home from school for most of John's friends, but not one of them had so much as walked up our garden path to ring the bell. No one had even phoned, although John kept his mobile charged up and ready for action twenty-four hours a day. Once I even caught him texting himself with my phone – how sad is that? But no one actually called.

It took me a while to notice what wasn't going on. John's not exactly unpopular, but he'd never been at the centre of any gang. He gets bored too easily, Mum says. "He's so far ahead of them he loses interest." That's probably true, though it wouldn't hurt if he was better at hiding the fact. After all, who loses out when no one wants to play with him? John Forster, that's who.

It was some weeks after the accident when it suddenly hit me that *no one* had been in to sign his plaster cast. Not even Rob – and Rob was the closest thing John had to a best friend.

"What's happened to little Rob?" I asked John one day. "Has he emigrated?"

"He's around," said John vaguely. As usual it wasn't easy to jemmy his attention from whatever he was thinking about at that moment. Just then he was tweaking a computer program he'd been writing on his laptop. It was a multiplayer version of *Hangman* called *Lynch Mob*, and John was sure it was going to make him millions.

"He's *not* around," I insisted. "And nor is anyone else. Look at your plaster cast! Where are all the signatures? It should be smothered in pictures and stupid jokes by now."

"I don't miss them," said John with a yawn. "Their loss, isn't it? I've got plenty to do."

He wasn't fooling anyone. I spotted him the next day as I came home from school, stationed on the sofa in my bay window and looking all puppy-dog forlorn with his face to the glass. I don't believe he was waiting for his big sister.

I know what the trouble was. Galder. I'm not sure how he was doing it, but he was the one stopping anyone from thinking of John. And when John's friends came up the street it was Galder walking them past our house as if it didn't exist. He wanted to keep John isolated, you see, away from anything that might stimulate him. Then, if John got frustrated enough, his imagination would boil over like a pan of milk and Galder would be there, ready to skim it off.

That's the way I see it now, of course. At the time I was just confused. It's hard to remember, but back then I didn't realize Galder wasn't alone. I hadn't even heard of the Lurkers. If I'd had the slightest idea what they were really up to, I'd already have—

But no. I've got to tell this story in the right order, just the way it happened. That's what I'm here to do.

Galder himself was around all this time; you can be sure of that, though he was keeping out of my way.

Me and Galder, we were the real enemies: I think we both recognized that from the start. No one else really saw what was happening. Even John was blind to it. I'm not saying I understood either, quite, not so I could put it into words the way I'm doing now, but one thing was clear to me: Galder was after my little brother. And that, I would not allow.

Meanwhile the wall of my room had eased back into place. It wasn't quite where it had been before, but it was near enough not to draw attention to itself. I didn't even bother telling Mum or Dad about it. I knew by now what they'd say. "Stop fussing, Verity – you've got a lovely room. You chose the wallpaper yourself."

Yes, I *know*, the wallpaper has nothing to do with it. That's my parents for you.

I didn't want to have to put them to the test, if you want to know. There was still a bit of me that wanted to think they were perfect and all-powerful. That belief had taken a battering over the years. No one who loses his specs quite as often as my father can keep up an aura of impregnable wisdom, and when your mum's a slave to every diet going (diced guava and spinach were big around then) you can't pretend she's immune to outside influence. But I couldn't bear to watch them let me down by denying what was so obvious – that John was being stolen from right under their noses.

The next Saturday I was drying my hair when the doorbell rang. Half a minute passed without anyone answering it. It rang again, more insistently. I wasn't alone in the house, but John wouldn't move that precious leg of his from the coffee table, and Dad had a curious habit of going deaf when the rugby was on, so I made a hasty towel-turban and went downstairs in my dressing gown, hoping this wouldn't be the day they sent a TV crew round to interview me about my top five style tips.

It wasn't, but it was someone just as unexpected. Milo Marsh, the crunch tackler.

"Hi," muttered Milo. He stood in the porch with his eyes downcast.

"Hi," I replied, trying to sound less astonished than I felt.

"Is your brother…is John…*all right*?" he asked, with exaggerated sincerity.

"He's much better," I said coolly. "No thanks to you."

"It wasn't my fault," began Milo in the same whiny voice I remembered from just after the accident. "I *had* to—"

"I know, I know. You'd got no choice, poor poppet. I remember."

Milo went red, and for a moment I thought he was going to thump me, but instead he thrust something into my hand. "I brought this," he said quickly.

I looked. It was a copy of the programme from last night's semi-final cup tie. Bristol Rovers versus

Chelsea. John had talked of nothing else at breakfast: Rovers had won 6–1. I turned it over gingerly, as if it might be booby-trapped.

"They've all signed it," said Milo. "The whole Rovers team."

"But where did you manage to get hold of—"

"My uncle works in security up there. I asked him specially. 'Cause of...you know." He shifted from foot to foot, as if he'd have liked to go now but didn't quite know how.

"Thanks." I peered at his face to see if I could detect some sniping mockery hidden there. "I'll give it to John. I'm sure he'll be pleased."

Milo seemed to take that as permission to leave. He nodded briefly, turned and scuttled down the garden path.

"Hang on!" I shouted. Milo hovered, with one hand latching the gate. "This match last night. Did you see it?"

"Course I did," he said. "Best night of my life. We

beat Chelsea all around the park. Wembley next! Wembley here we come..."

His voice went all dreamy then. I didn't like to wake him, so I watched him cross the street, with his head stuck inside a Wembley-shaped dream-cloud. When he reached the far pavement he stopped and shook himself and peered around him, as if he didn't recognize where he was. He patted his pockets, obviously looking for something, but couldn't find it – then he gave up, kicked a can in disgust, and clomped off down the road, hands stuffed in the pockets of his low-slung jeans.

Maybe someone with a few more brain cells to spare than Milo Marsh might have wondered longer how it was that he had wound up outside our door minus his precious programme – and why his mind was a blank. But Milo was used to his mind being blank. That was normal for him. Even so, it frightened me all over again. If Galder was behind this (and I knew he *was*) it showed just how much power he had. It wasn't only a matter of bending Milo Marsh to his will – conquering a mind the size of a pin doesn't really count for much in the Evil Genius stakes – but Bristol Rovers and Chelsea? *6–1?* I don't take much notice of football, but even I knew that was…odd.

On the other hand, why not? I'd been seeing the newspaper headlines all over Bristol for a while, of course, as Rovers had made their unlikely progress through the competition: "Rovers Jack Up Giant-Killing Hopes", and so on. The school was buzzing with it. And I knew that every year there's some team of non-league Sunday scuffers who bring a millionaire club to its knees. Why shouldn't it be Bristol Rovers' turn for glory this year? Perhaps I was being silly, after all.

Whatever lay behind Milo's visit, the effect on John was amazing. When I showed him the programme he stared at it goggle-eyed.

"This," he croaked, "is gold dust!"

"Glad you're pleased," I said. I couldn't see why he was quite *so* excited about a programme for a match that had already happened. Still, it was good to see John being enthusiastic about something for a change.

"The magic of the Cup, that's what it is! Rob is going to be so jealous when he sees this."

"I'm sure he would be," I said sharply, "if he came round any more."

That was a bit unkind. But I was bothered by the way Rob and the rest of John's so-called friends had abandoned him. And I was cross with John for pretending not to care.

John looked at me reproachfully, as if Rob's non-appearance was *my* fault. "He'll be round," he said. "You fuss too much. Why don't you go and live your own life, and stop poking your nose into mine?"

I do have a life of my own, of course – when I'm allowed to. I told you at the start, I don't have much time to write this story down, and that means there's a lot of stuff I'm leaving out, things that have nothing to do with John or Galder. I actually have a very full social diary, what with choir and netball and the swimming club. I may not be the most popular girl in class – my truth-telling habit has seen to that – but I do have Gina, Jen and Sally (when she's not in love with some leathery biker), and Juanita of the Colgate smile. The point is they don't belong in this story.

Actually, though, it was Juanita who first tipped me off that Galder was on the move again. She's as sensitive as a cat, and since she's been wearing a brace on her teeth it's been worse. She seems to pick up radio signals from some other dimension on it.

It happened that very afternoon. Juanita had come over to watch a DVD. In she sauntered, flashing that titanium grin. "Got the crisps?"

She yoiked her bag over the bannister and bounded up the stairs. But at the top I saw her flinch, as if someone had flicked a wet towel in her face. It was when she passed the airing cupboard. She pressed herself against the wall. Her brace glinted distantly in the sudden shadow.

"Something wrong?" I asked as I caught her up.

"What's living in *there*?" she asked, pointing to the cupboard. I swear to you, her teeth were chattering, metal brace and all.

My first thought was for Jump Jet Harry. If any dog is capable of locking himself in an airing cupboard, he's it. But I could hear him downstairs just then, nagging Dad for a walk.

"Nothing. What are you talking about?"

"I heard something, Verity. Scratching. And the *stink*!" Juanita twisted her nose in disgust. "Can't you smell it?"

"For goodness' sake!" I snapped. I had enough to deal with, without Juanita getting an attack of the vapours. I opened the airing cupboard. "Look, there's nothing there. No smell. Nothing worse than Mum's fabric conditioner, anyway. That's pretty sick-making, I'll grant you." Piled along the slatted shelves were the neatly-folded towels and sheets in various feng shui-friendly colours. It was all mind-numbingly ordinary.

Juanita looked a bit sheepish. "Sorry. But something round here is dead creepy."

I shut the cupboard door and led her into my bedroom, trying to persuade myself that everything was normal. Juanita hadn't seen anything. She hadn't even claimed to see anything. But I couldn't shut out the memory of a certain…*shudder* in the air just as the door was closing, as if something very cautious were shrinking back amongst the fitted sheets, boiling itself down to a pool of clotted shadow. I sensed that shadow, making itself small and inconspicuous with the dust and dead spiders, trying to be as near to nothing as it could. If I'd been someone else I might easily have blinked, and put it out of my head. But I'm Verity. It's a curse. And soon, I'd understand it all too well.

Meanwhile, the visitations began. Juanita and I were eating a post-movie soup 'n' chip dip in the kitchen (it's our favourite) when the doorbell rang. I got up to answer, and found little Rob standing there.

"Hello, Verity," he said. "I've come to visit John. May I come in?"

Now, if you knew Rob you'd realize just how weird this was. Normally he hardly waits for the door to be opened a crack before he's pushing past and making for the stairs, with nothing but a discarded coat on the hall floor to show where he's been. The polite boy on the doorstep *looked* like Rob, but—

"May I come in?" he repeated, without a hint of sarcasm.

"Be my guest," I said, feeling puzzled.

Rob came in. He took his trainers off carefully, untying his laces: I didn't think he knew how. He hung his coat neatly on the stand, and walked – not ran – upstairs. Stunned, I returned to Juanita in the kitchen and dunked an extra-long chip into the soup. "Boys are just crazy," I said.

"Tell me about it," Juanita sighed.

Rob was up there half an hour. Juanita had just left, and I was rinsing the dishes in the kitchen when I heard him in the hall again. "Off so soon?" I called. I didn't know what was going on, but I was determined to find out. I went back to the hall.

"Thank you for having me," said Rob, tying the laces of his trainers neatly with a double bow. "It's been lovely."

"Good grief, Rob! Where do you think you are, Buckingham Palace?"

He looked blank then, as if he didn't understand what Buckingham Palace was. Or rather, as if I'd strayed from a script and he was having to *ad lib* a reply. "This house is a palace to me," he said finally, in the same tone of earnest blankness. "As long as it contains that paragon of friendship and good company, John Forster."

All right. That was it. Everything until then might – just *might* – have been down to an unexpected burst of good behaviour. Maybe Rob's parents were bribing him with a puppy, or doping his cornflakes. But "paragon"? Even I wasn't sure what that meant. There was no way Rob Barley, who had never in his life read anything longer than the menu at McDonald's, was going to know a paragon from a parakeet.

"Galder!" I said, catching him by the scruff of the neck. "He's put you up to this, hasn't he?"

"Galder?" said Rob mildly. Not a question, not a denial, not an admission. Just a word.

"Yes! Come on, tell the truth!"

He stared up at me. He didn't answer, or fight, or struggle to get free. Just waited.

I gave up and pushed him away. "All right," I announced to the house in general. "I know you're around, Galder. Whatever dimension you've slipped into, I know you're there. You're not fooling anyone."

"Don't shout, Miss Verity," said Rob. "Who knows what you might wake, that would be better left slumbering?"

"Shut up, you!"

Rob looked pained. "I hadn't thought to see such violence in you. That's not the way, you know, not the way at all."

"Galder – is that *you*?"

For Rob's round face had suddenly seemed to blur and spread like melting butter…

Then it snapped back into position.

"I don't know anyone by that name," said Rob, letting himself out through the front door. I watched as he reached the gate and turned left towards the shops. For a moment I was too shocked to move. Then I ran after him. The road stretched away in both directions. But Rob was not on it.

"I told you my friends would be coming round," said John triumphantly, appearing on the stairs behind me. "I expect there'll be others before long." Saying this he smothered an elaborate yawn and ran his fingers aground as he tried to smooth his knotted hair. He looked awful. Although I'd seen him fifty times a day, I hadn't really taken in the change in him until then. Now, though, I saw him as Rob (if it had *been* Rob) must have seen him, set against the John of the month before. It didn't make pretty viewing. His eyelids drooped like wilted daffodils, and all his features were dingy in the orange landing light.

"God, John, you look like death warmed up."

"Thanks," said John indifferently. "Fancy a go on my new PlayStation game, later? It's a two-hander."

The next boy at the door was Karim, the football captain. I didn't know him well, so it was hard to tell if he was acting out of character, but he was all "How is John today?" and "May I have the honour of a visit?" and "I took the liberty of bringing a small gift – a mere token." How many Year Six children talk like that, I'd like to know? If someone was trying to fool me into thinking all this was normal, they weren't making much of an effort. Then it was up the stairs – carefully removing his shoes first, just like Rob – and twenty minutes in John's room and out again, with elaborate goodbyes. This time Mum was there to see him go.

"What do *you* think of all this?" I asked her, wondering how much she'd actually noticed.

"Of what, Verity?"

"All these weeks John's had no visitors at all, and now he's had three in one day. Doesn't that strike you as just a little *odd*?"

"Good, isn't it?" said Mum, as if she were agreeing. "I'm pleased John has such a loyal set of friends. And so polite!"

"Hmph! It's like he's holding court in there. King Arthur and his pint-sized knights!"

Mum gave one of her ironical laughs. "I don't understand you at all, Verity. For weeks you've been complaining about John moping, and as soon as he manages to kick-start his social life you're not happy about that either!"

I noticed, however, that Mum made herself pretty scarce for the rest of the day. Suddenly it was essential to clear out the greenhouse and do an inventory of potting trays – and from there you can't hear the doorbell. So it was me who had to open the door each time it rang. It rang a lot. Every twenty minutes or so they came, a series of boys, and one or two girls as well, mostly from John's class. Always one at a time. Always polite. Always staying about quarter of an hour then going on their orderly way. It was getting monotonous.

I began to notice something else about these polite, half-familiar strangers. Their eyes. Their eyes bothered me, and at first I wasn't sure why. Then I realized it was the way they lingered, a little too long and unblinkingly – staring the way a baby stares, bold and unashamed, like people who haven't learned the knack of being embarrassed yet. Was there anybody behind those eyes? The more I watched, the more I was convinced there was not. And their

CHAPTER 5

John didn't answer my knock. I opened the door and went into his room, surprised to find the curtains shut against the sun.

"Who is it this time?" asked John with a mixture of fatigue and irritation. He didn't even look round from his computer.

"Expecting anyone in particular?"

When he heard my voice he seemed, for a moment, almost pleased to see me. Relieved rather than pleased, perhaps. "With Galder, who knows?"

"I see. You do realize, then?"

"Huh?"

"About these so-called friends of yours."

Something big-sisterish in my tone must have irked him because he snapped back, "What do you mean, 'so-called'? They're great friends. They talk sense. And they go away when you don't want them around any more," he added meaningfully.

But I wasn't about to be put off. "I didn't even recognize the last boy who came."

"Sean from my old nursery," he said. "We used to have tricycle races in the playground – twice round the holly tree. I haven't seen him since we were four."

It took a minute for this to sink in. "Sean from your nursery, eh? You haven't seen him in years, and then he turns up, right on cue. That's remarkable."

"If you say so."

"Hmmm. John, did you mention anything to Galder about this friend Sean of yours?"

"I don't know!" said John. "Ask him! What are you getting at?"

"I'm not sure, yet. It's just – where are all these friends coming from?"

John shrugged, but he did not meet my eye. "I guess Galder knows me pretty well."

The air crackled at this. Suddenly the room had the colour sucked from it, and the light that was left was flickering somehow. I could *feel* Galder nearby.

And Galder was there. You couldn't say that he appeared out of thin air, exactly. It was more a question of being there all the time, and choosing only now to let his "thereness" show. "Right enough," he said, as his body seeped into space like an ink blot. "Always listening, always attentive to your will, young Master John."

"See?" said John to me. He seemed to think he had

proved a point. "But I'd like a rest now, Galder. Lay off with the friends for a bit."

"Of course," agreed Galder with a quick bow. "Just as soon as you've seen your last visitor."

"No, Galder. That's enough. I don't want any more."

"But your visitor is already here, young master. In the house. You surely don't want to turn away your oldest and dearest friend? The companion of your youth? The first you ever loved?" Galder smiled a fatherly smile.

Now John was puzzled. So was I.

"Who do you mean? What friend?" he demanded. "Someone else from my nursery, is it? Not Sharyn May, the girl with the hair like a bell rope?"

"What's wrong with Sharyn May?" I asked. John looked so horrified I almost laughed.

"We got engaged under the art table when we were nearly four. I don't think I ever called it off!"

"Don't be ridiculous. Sharyn will have forgotten all

about you by now," I said. But something in that smile of Galder's was making my stomach curdle.

"You need not worry on that score, Master John," said Galder. "Your sister's right – the human heart is fickle. But you're neglecting someone else. A friend who has waited faithfully all these years."

Was it my imagination? Or did I hear a small mewing sigh at that moment? A muffled pawing of cloth on wood, just outside the door?

I looked at John. He seemed uneasy and confused. But he guessed the truth before I did.

"Louis…"

Galder swept his arm towards the bedroom door with a stately motion, the gesture bringing a wind in its wake that pushed the door wide open. We could all see onto the landing. And the thing on the landing – the little figure with felt eyes and coathanger fingernails, standing with the airing-cupboard door open behind it – that thing could see us too.

"*Want play!*" it said.

It spoke with a voice I had not heard for six years. It took a moment to place it. Then I knew it was John's voice, as it had been long ago, even before his engagement to Sharyn May. King Arthur had been no more than a name in those days. The Turbo Heroes had yet to face the Mitron Troopers for the first time. John's world had been bounded by Mum and Dad and me. And good old Louis Patooey.

"Want play!" said Louis Patooey. "*Now!*"

Louis was small. Not small enough to fit in John's satchel, the way he'd done in the old days, but I don't think he came higher than John's waist. He seemed to be wearing a pair of John's pyjamas, with the trousers rolled up clumsily. I'd never seen anyone so bizarre – yet he was familiar too, in unexpected ways. His lime-coloured face, his hands the colour of ripe plums, the strange mottled texture of his feet and mouth – even the faint scent that drifted from him reminded me of, of, what? Pine woods? Green, spiky needles? Where had I smelled that before? His face was smooth and blank, as if all the life and movement in it had been pressed out through years of clothy stillness. His eyes were just sewn-on patches of black felt. Only his mouth was mobile, with thin, dry lips that pursed and swagged as the words came yet again. "Want play! *Now!*"

A scar, barely visible before, twitched and throbbed in his face as he spoke. From the side of the throat and diagonally up across his face it ran, curling like a question mark around one ear. It was horrible.

John was terrified. Too terrified even to back away from Louis Patooey when he started walking towards him, lisping: "Play! Play!"

I grabbed at Louis as he passed, but let go at once. The touch of his skin was repellent. That mottled skin was not skin at all, but cloth, dry and yielding and cotton soft, but with a fibrous strength. And that smell – I had it now – was Mum's *Pine Glade* fabric conditioner. The throbbing scar was no more than the seam of a pillow, inside out, with the loose stitches showing.

"Galder!" I yelled, as Louis Patooey padded towards John. "Get rid of it! Now!"

"Not without the young master's say-so," said Galder. "I wouldn't presume."

Until this point Louis's movements had been slow, a little clumsy, but now with a sudden agility he ran forward and embraced John's knees in obvious rapture. Six years' desire to play with John were concentrated in that gesture.

"Johnny! Johnny play Louis now!"

John was too frightened to speak. He kept looking around for help from Galder. But Galder was suddenly nowhere to be seen.

"John, you have to talk to him!"

John made a great effort. "Yes, Louis," he said, gasping between each word. "Yes, we'll play. That's what you want? What game would you like?"

Louis's cloth face went a deeper shade of lime.

His mouth swagged in a foolish grin.

"Twain!" he lisped tenderly. "Choo twain!"

With that he took a leap, and, with a power I would never have expected from his doughy legs, sprang towards John's throat. John ducked, but in a flash Louis Patooey's arms were locked around his neck, with Louis himself riding piggyback and lisping joyously: "Twain! Louis wide! Choo, choo!"

The whistle of a steam train blew eerily from his mouth.

"Stop – it!" gasped John, staggering forward on his cast. "I – can't *breathe*!"

"Louis wide on twain!" hooted Louis Patooey, jiggling on John's back. Somehow he managed to keep his grip on John's throat with one hand, while with the other he waved happily to me, each finger tipped with a nail of curved coathanger wire. "Wide Johnny!"

John said through gritted teeth: "Get – *off*!"

"Wide Johnny now!" cried Louis Patooey, tightening his polyester-cotton grip.

"Play with him, for goodness' sake, John! Be a train! Go chug-a-chug-a-chug!"

John chugged. Splutteringly. He jog-hobbled around the room, half-bent under the weight of Louis Patooey (who must have been far heavier than he looked), and flailing his arms in desperate imitation of a piston.

Louis, at any rate, was delighted. "Fast! Make twain fast!"

"I can't go any faster!" yelped John. Then he added cunningly, "Let's swap places now. Louis Patooey be train and Johnny ride! It'll be fun!"

But Louis wasn't having any of it. Something told me that when he and John played together in the old days John would have bagged all the best parts for himself. Louis was making up for it now.

"Louis wide twain fast!" he declared. And he looped his fabric-soft arm still tighter round John's neck, smiling broadly.

I wish I'd never seen that smile. It wasn't that

Louis's teeth were so very sharp. But who expects to see a set of plastic clothes pegs filling someone's mouth? Mum had left them in the airing cupboard, I suppose. Now his mouth was a red, green, yellow, blue and purple grin, and along the centre of each tooth shone a horizontal wire from the spring of the peg, gleaming like Juanita's brace.

No wonder the kid had trouble with his "r"s. It made him look kind of sad and home-made, as well as scary – like a craft project gone wrong. But that didn't stop him twisting his limbs round and round on themselves, as if he were being wrung out, until they were tight as muscles, choking the breath from John.

John was going purple now. I rushed to pull at Louis, desperately trying to prise his pad-like hand from John's throat.

"Get off, you! Bad! Bad boy!"

"Twain," lisped Louis Patooey relentlessly, grinning his rainbow grin. And he turned and spat a green clothes peg into my eye.

I blinked away the sharp pain. I had to get Louis off John's throat. Looking around I found John's *Star Wars* lightsaber on the bed. I brought it down – *thwump!* – on Louis Patooey's head.

He didn't take the slightest bit of notice. He just clung on to John with his soft mottled fingers. His wire nails curved like talons into John's neck. John had collapsed. A few more seconds and he'd be unconscious. His eyes met mine, then moved to the lightsaber, and flickered weakly.

At once I heard a *whoof* sound beside me, as if a gas jet had just ignited. The lightsaber was glowing! Not with the shoddy twenty-watt glow it used to have before the battery inside went flat. This was the full works. It had to be Galder's doing.

"All right," I said to Louis Patooey. "Chew on this!"

I slashed at Louis's head. And through it. And out the other side. The room was instantly filled with the smell of burned polyester-cotton sheets.

I was looking down at the ruins of Mum's laundry. Where my lightsaber had sliced, the edge of the material still smoked. A scatter of plastic clothes pegs lay about the floor. I tossed the lightsaber back onto the bed. Already it was no more than a cheap toy from Woolworths once again.

"Are you okay, John?" I asked.

"I think so," he spluttered.

"You ought to choose your friends more carefully," I said as he got his breath back. I wasn't talking about Louis Patooey.

You've got to hand it to John. Most kids in that situation would have been blubbing with fear. I felt like crying myself, now the danger was past. My hand was shaking. But John was up at once, and a minute later he was shouting. "Galder! Show yourself right now!"

"John, calm down!" I said.

"I know you're there, Galder. I know you can hear me!"

I started to kick the pile of charred bedsheets that had been Louis Patooey under the bed. It was ridiculous, but in the state I was in I could think of nothing but that Mum might come in and blame me for the mess.

"Can I be of assistance?" purred Galder in the doorway.

I hadn't been sure what to expect, or even if Galder would materialize at all, just because John wanted him to. But there he was, as servile as ever, bowing so deeply that you could trace the greasy furrow of his parted hair all the way from his forehead to the nape of his neck. "Why, Master John, you seem distressed."

"You bet your life I'm distressed! What did you mean by bringing Louis Patooey to life? He nearly killed me!"

Galder pretended to be surprised, but he didn't pretend very hard. "I had thought that was your wish, young master. To be visited by your friends."

"My friends *now*, I meant. My living, breathing friends!"

"You did not specify—"

"I shouldn't need to, not to you! If anyone knows what I mean it's –"

John bit his lip, with a sharp look at me, as if there was something he hadn't wanted to say in front of me. Then he decided not to care, he was so angry.

"You knew just what I wanted. You've been reading my mind long enough, Galder, you can't deny it."

"And fascinating reading it makes too, Master John. A real page-turner."

"You'd no right!"

"You have suffered no wrong by it, Master John. How else could I be sure what you truly desired? Besides, it was my power that allowed Miss Verity to rid you of that poor neglected creature. I am always watching over you, you see?"

John opened his mouth to protest, then stopped.

For at that moment Galder had decided once again not to be there any more.

I knelt down beside the ruins of Louis Patooey and started collecting the bundle of sheets. I put as many of the plastic clothes pegs as I could find into my pocket. What I had just seen and heard had left me dazed – but somehow I didn't feel too surprised.

"I was here to help you this time, John," I said, though I knew he wasn't listening. A seared strip of lime-coloured fabric hung from my hand, still with the patch of black felt that had been Louis Patooey's eye. "Don't you think you'd better stop this now? Next time someone's going to end up getting fried."

CHAPTER 6

John didn't know *how* to stop by this time, of course. But I think that was the first time he had had to face it – the fact that he'd lost control. I told you at the beginning that John was clever, but he can be pretty stupid, too. Maybe you've noticed that by now. Stupid in a clever way, of course: he can always come up with a reason why he's right and you're wrong.

Anyone would think it gave him physical pain, admitting he doesn't know something.

That's why it took him so long, I suppose, to admit that Galder wasn't his devoted slave. Why he'd ever thought a magical servant would pop up out of nowhere to do his bidding is a mystery, but I think John reckoned he was worth it. And when it happened, he wasn't about to rock the boat. But now, the weather was starting to get rough. The boat was rocking *him*.

This would have been the perfect time for John to come clean, confess he was in over his head, and ask his big sister for help.

Fat chance. Instead, he withdrew: from me, Mum, Dad – everyone. Even my parents noticed. For instance, every Friday evening he and Dad used to play shoot-'em-ups on his PlayStation. They'd done it for years, keeping a running tally that filled three exercise books. Something to do with male bonding, I suppose. Not any more.

"I'm getting too old for that now, Dad," said John, when Dad started hooking up the machine after supper. "Hadn't you noticed?"

Dad looked forlorn. *He* obviously wasn't too old for it. But John was already off up to his room, checking out something on the Internet. He spent a lot of time up there these days.

John should have been back at school long since, of course. Lots of people totter around on crutches, after all. Galder, however, had arranged things differently. Whenever John saw the doctor she would smile encouragingly and say how well the break was mending.

"Do you think he'll be able to go back to school soon?" Mum would ask hopefully. The school where she worked had been pretty understanding about giving her time off, but they were getting impatient. "We're keen for him not to fall too far behind."

"Of course," the doctor began, "it will be good for him to get out and –"

Then the doctor's face would go vague and fuddled, and she'd be searching for the right words, and the right words weren't there any more, and out would come Galder's words instead: "I think we'd better play safe and keep him off just a little longer. These fractures can be very tricky."

And Mum, who'd never dream of questioning a doctor, could do nothing but agree.

None of this happened very long ago. But so many things were going on about then that it's hard for me to know what order to tell them in. Some I hardly noticed, I was so wrapped up in my own worries. They didn't seem to have anything to do with John or Galder – just the world being crazy in its own weird way. But looking back from where I am now it's all clear. Now I'm like someone standing on a hillside, looking at a battle on the plain down below. I can see how the different parts of the action connect up. At the time, it was just chaos.

For instance, there was the man in the shopping centre that Saturday. I'd seen him before, a long-haired preacher, in tinted glasses and a shabby coat, banging on about Jesus. I'd always thought he was a little crazy, but harmless enough. He loved telling us how we were all destined for hell, and about the agonies waiting for us there. "You are the Devil's porters!" he would cry, looking along the rows of carrier bags from Miss Selfridge and House of Fraser and Next. "These are the badges of your vanity, and they shall be your passport to the everlasting fire!" I didn't much care for the relish with which he said it, but I couldn't help feeling a bit sorry for him, the way everyone just smirked and walked on past.

Not today, though. Today they were hooked. Those wicked carrier bags were lying abandoned on the pavement, with neatly folded dresses, tops, and DVDs spilling onto the ground.

"The end is at hand!" said the preacher. "I hear the

thunder of His chariot wheels, I feel the beat of His wings upon the air!"

No one smirked. No one moved. Somewhere in the crowd I heard a woman give a whimper of fear.

"You cry out now," said the preacher. "But you are too late! All too late." He gave a smug, lingering smile as he looked us up and down. "If you had only acted in the spring! Now the wheat stands blasted in the fields, and the harvest is lost. You are going to the place where there is wailing and gnashing of teeth, freezing fire and scalding cold."

It was colourful stuff, but no different from what he threatened us with every week. The difference was that now he had an audience.

"What shall we do?" called out a woman a little way behind me. "Lord forgive us!" wailed another. The preacher didn't look at all surprised. He'd obviously been expecting that this day would come. I scanned the faces of the crowd. They all wore the same expressions: anxious, scared, guilty. Even that tall lad in the leather jacket, who – who was –

No! It couldn't be!

Milo Marsh?

But it *was* Milo, with tears washing his cheeks and dripping onto his trainers.

A repentant Milo Marsh was too much to take. I hurried on towards the shops, bought the new top I'd come to town for, and took the bus home as soon as I could. Even so, I was aware of people staring at me on the top deck. I heard the whispers: "Fancy!" they were saying. "Buying herself fripperies, as if there was no tomorrow!"

"People are acting kind of weird out there," I said to my mother when I got home. "Some of them seem to think the end of the world is just around the corner."

"You shouldn't mock people's beliefs," said my mother primly.

"But they're saying –" I began. Then I decided not to bother. Mum had her closed face on: I knew I'd get no more out of her. Besides, there was more to this than an attack of religion. Even at the shopping centre I'd half-wondered whether this doomsday fear might have something to do with Galder. The suspicion had been itching at the back of my mind, waiting for me to scratch it.

I scratched it now. And saw I'd been an idiot. A moron. All this time I'd been trying to protect my stupid brother. I'd been so focused on him I hadn't looked beyond the walls of our own house. Of course, I'd known Galder *could* affect what went on in the world outside. There was the matter of the two-Sundays-in-a-row to prove that. But that had been connected straight back to John, trying to prove himself to me as usual. It was the same when Bristol Rovers got through to the FA Cup Final – out of nowhere. That was just the kind of thing John would have wished for. But the end of the world? John had never been religious, not a bit of it. No way would he be wanting mad preachers to forecast doomsday. If

Galder was involved, he had to be doing it on his own initiative. But why? What was Galder trying to do?

John was watching daytime telly, as usual. He was switching channels every few seconds. Flick-flick-flick. Maybe he didn't even know he was doing it. *Classic Lottery Draws*, *Soccer Rodeo*, *Celebrity Sofas*: John wasn't stopping for any of it. Just flick-flick-flick, with his other hand straying occasionally into a nearby box of Maltesers. In between flicks he saw me come in, but didn't look up. He could probably tell I meant business.

"I was watching that!" he squealed when I turned the television off.

"Not any more. We've got to talk, John. Now!" He opened his mouth to protest, but I was too quick for him. "I don't know what kind of deal you think you've got going with Galder, but I can guess. Your own personal genie, was that the idea? Your every wish is his command? Was that what he offered you?"

"Something like that," he replied, feeling about for the TV remote. I could see he was still trying to pretend I wasn't there.

"Then what's happened? Look at yourself, John! You're turning into a mindless slob. You can't concentrate on anything for more than a couple of seconds. The only exercise you get is changing channel."

He turned slowly, and looked at me with heavy contempt. "You think you've got the whole thing figured out, don't you? You stand there looking down on it all from that high perch of yours. Verity Who Tells It Like It Is. That's right, isn't it? Don't think I don't see."

"That's not fair!"

"But you don't know a thing about Galder. Who he is. *What* he is."

"So tell me!"

"Okay," he sighed, "you obviously aren't going to get there on your own. Watch this."

He pushed a button on the TV remote. The screen flickered and a moment later I was staring at thick green jungle. It was one of those nature programmes, and sure enough there was John's favourite presenter, squatting in front of some apes.

"Our ancestors," the presenter was saying, in a breathy whisper. "So near to being human. Yet no ape ever looked up at the stars and wondered what it meant to be alive. No ape ever pondered the meaning of its own existence. No ape ever made a television series." (The presenter allowed himself a smile, here.) "What happened to our own ape ancestors to make *them* become *us*?"

"This is all very interesting, John, but—"

"Shh!"

Now the presenter looked very serious and puzzled. His brow furrowed. Even his hair furrowed. And greased. And blackened. He leaned forward a little and clasped his hands obsequiously. "What happened," he said, "was the Lurkers."

The presenter now bore a striking resemblance to Galder himself.

"Where did they come from?" Galder continued, still using his breathy presenter's voice. "Nobody knows. Even the Lurkers themselves have forgotten, in their long wanderings through time and space. Past millions of planets they drifted, and on each they sought out living creatures with whom to share their existence. Not any life would do. Only life with the rudiments of intelligence would make fit soil for them to plant themselves. Their journey was long, but at last they came upon a blue planet near the edge of the Milky Way. Earth. There they found a species of ape that fitted their needs perfectly. Intelligent and curious, these apes already had a sense of beauty. They already dreamed at night. But when they awoke, what became of those dreams?" Galder snapped his fingers. "They disappeared like bubbles surfacing on a pond."

Galder looked out of the screen with a look of

benevolent pity. "But help was at hand. The Lurkers made their homes in these ape-minds. From the apes they received shelter and companionship. But the apes themselves gained far more. The Lurkers gave them the blessing of self-awareness. In the Lurkers they had a mirror in which to see themselves, and a voice in which to think their thoughts. The Lurkers allowed humanity to become...*human*. Without the Lurkers," added Galder more aggressively, "you'd still be picking fleas out of each other's hair and sucking termites off sticks."

I'd had enough of this. "Yeah, right!" I switched the TV off. "What are you saying? That we've got these...*Lurker* things living inside our heads?"

"That's right," smiled John. "We all have. Resident aliens. Pure mental life forms. That's what Galder is."

"Right – like I need some alien slimeball to see myself in the mirror!"

"Calm down!" cried John. "It's natural history. A bit of history no one knows except me – and now you. You see it? All this time you've been so down on Galder. Don't you realize you should actually be grateful? That's what his kind has done for the human race. They *made* it."

"Got you well trained, hasn't he? You really believe that?"

"It happens all the time in nature. Symbiosis, they call it. Two creatures living together, each gives the other something it needs. Think of the bacteria in your guts. You give them somewhere to live, they help you digest your food. Beautiful. The Lurkers are no different."

"All right, all right! But if Galder's kind likes cosying up inside people's minds, how come I can *see* him? What's he doing outside a nice, safe human host? Tell me that!"

"I will if you let me," said John. "I told you at the beginning Galder was a refugee. The truth is," he added in a confidential whisper, "he had a bad experience, five hundred years ago."

That took me by surprise, I admit. "Galder's that old?" He didn't look much over forty.

John tapped his head. "Mental life form, see? Not physical. Weren't you listening? Why should they die just because their host's body wears out? They move on and find a new one. Obvious when you think about it."

It was the matter-of-fact way he said it that got to me. Standing there listening to my little brother spout this stuff I felt as if I'd lurched back to the shopping centre and that wild-eyed preacher man. John wasn't wild-eyed, but he had the same utter conviction in what he was saying. It was as if someone else was standing at his shoulder with a prompt book, ready to cue him every time he faltered. He was very convincing, too. But then I'm a bit contrary like that. The more convincing he became, the less I believed a word of it.

"One of his hosts, see, was a great scholar. A magician – or that's how he thought of himself.

Somehow he became aware of Galder. For a Lurker that's the worst possible thing."

"I can imagine," I said sarcastically. "Embarrassing or what!"

"This man didn't understand the whole truth, of course. He thought Galder was a spirit, a demon. He was bound to see it like that, living back then. He tried to conjure him up, using Latin books and chalk circles. He had this idea of making him a slave, to do even more powerful magic for him." John stopped distractedly, as if he was listening to someone whisper instructions in his ear.

"And did he succeed?" I asked.

"You've seen what Galder is like. He got stuck halfway. He's not of the mind, not of the body: he can't find rest in either form. He has no real place at all. That's how it was, anyway, until I came along. I tried to help him."

This sounded like baloney to me. "I can see what *you* get out of it," I said. "Someone to fetch and carry, to rearrange the world the way you want it. But what about him?"

"I told you. I give him…shelter. He can't live by himself all the time – he'd dry out, like a frog in the desert. I give him a place to stay, to rest, to recharge his batteries. In here." He tapped his head. "It's quite luxurious. A first-class mind, Galder says. A penthouse suite of a brain. That's what he gets out of it. He *grazes*, I guess you could call it, on my spare ideas."

"You mean you let him – *that* – into your head? You're crazy!"

"Don't get so stressed, Verity. It's a good deal for us both. I've got enough ideas for two."

At that moment I was so angry with John I could hardly speak. Someone as clever as him has no right to be so stupid: it's an abuse of privilege. I tried – I tried very hard – to remember that he was also only a ten-year-old boy. The eyes looking back at me were John's. That irritating smirk was his. But I was no longer sure what mind lay behind either of them. John's? Or Galder's? I hoped there was still a difference.

"It makes perfect sense," he was saying. "If I didn't let Galder see a little way into my mind he'd have no way of knowing what I wanted him to do next. He'd never be able to surprise me. I like surprises."

"Like Louis Patooey, you mean?"

"Louis Patooey?" John grimaced. "That was just...overenthusiasm. Galder made a guess about what I'd like and got it wrong, that's all. Anyone can make a mistake, you know. And I could have called Louis Patooey off any time I wanted. You fuss too much, Verity."

I bit my lip and tried to ignore this. "Okay," I said. "Let's leave Louis Patooey out of it. What's this about the end of the world? Skiving off school is one thing. Being the most popular boy in town, I can see the appeal. Bristol Rovers as FA Cup winners? I can even get my head round that concept. But the

Apocalypse? Doomsday? Total destruction? Call me narrow-minded, but I just can't see what that's got going for it."

John frowned. "I don't know what you're talking about."

"You don't? Try going into town! It's all teeth-gnashing and wailing there, haven't you heard? I even saw Milo Marsh confessing his sins."

John laughed out loud. "Milo Marsh!"

"He was crying and asking for forgiveness."

"Milo crying? It would almost be worth having the end of the world to see *that*!"

"It wasn't funny, John. It was pathetic, and, well, scary."

"Since when was Milo Marsh *not* scary?"

"You don't get it—"

"None of this was anything to do with me, anyway. Maybe Galder's having some fun of his own. He likes tricks. Who knows?"

How could John discuss Galder as if he wasn't

right there with us, listening to every word we said? It seemed weird that he could forget about Galder with one part of his mind, even when he was talking about him. Weird – but, well, people *are* weird. Maybe our brains just aren't wired up to think about things like that. Things like the Lurkers, I mean, that you can't see and touch most of the time. That's why this story is so hard to write down. My eye keeps sliding off to left or right, to what happened next or just before, and who said what about it. I keep wanting to explain things in different ways. Rational ways. Crazy ones. Maybe I'm crazy myself, as John so helpfully suggested.

Even so: "Galder does *not* like tricks," I said. "Except when he can get something out of it. He's not a fun guy, you get that? He's wall-to-wall trouble. He's not on your side, John!"

John just looked at me. I could have counted to ten while he looked at me. His face gave away nothing.

"Okay," he said. "You've made your point. You

don't like Galder. I do. We'll both have to live with it. Anything else you wanted to say?"

"Yes! No! That is, give me a minute!"

"You know where to find me," he said, yawning.

Flick-flick-flick. John was changing channels again. I was off air.

I stomped into the kitchen. In a situation like this there was only one thing to do, and I did it. Within minutes I was eating a thick-sliced bacon sandwich. Stupid John, I thought as I chewed. And where had my parents got to? Mum might refuse to see that anything was wrong, but Dad – I think he's got a bit of Truth Hound in him too. He has to think things through to the end, just like me. It's probably something to do with being a lawyer.

But Dad wasn't around. He'd been late home from work every night that week. Even when he was in, he had no energy to do much beyond complaining about the case he'd been working on.

"It was meant to be a simple matter of

conveyancing," he began that evening at dinner. "St. Benedict's Chapel, as was. They're going to convert it into a nightclub – *Spires* – would you believe? Daft name. Then, just as we're about to exchange contracts, along comes a group of drifters and takes up residence. Now they're claiming squatters' rights!"

"Well, it was intended to be a house of God," said Mum with an air of pious reproof. "Shouldn't the homeless be sheltered? I'm sure the Bible says that somewhere."

"That's hardly the point," said Dad. He looked at her in surprise, because it was an odd thing for Mum to say. Mum is not usually a religious person at all. She hadn't been to church for as long as I could remember, unless you count her annual pilgrimage to the school nativity play. I could guess where she'd got her new-found interest, though. The religious fervour sweeping the shopping centre had clearly spread as far as our house.

I had to wait until the advert break in *News at Ten*

to get Dad's attention. John was in bed by then, and Mum was having a luxurious soak in something herbal.

"Dad?"

He jumped awake. He'd obviously been dozing, despite appearing to pay minute attention to the latest trade figures. It's a useful skill in his line of work. "Yes. What is it, Verity?"

"Would you say I was a level-headed sort of person?"

"Of course, love," Dad yawned.

"Not someone who lets her imagination carry her away?"

"Not beyond reason. I think you have as good a claim as any of us to being relatively sane. Why do you ask?"

"I just want to make sure you take me seriously. You do take me seriously, don't you?"

"Of course I do."

"Good. Well then, I'm worried about John."

"His leg, you mean? That's very thoughtful, Verity,

but you don't have to. It's just taking longer to heal than we expected."

"Not his leg! It's – it's more – it's all about –"

I tried to tell Dad about Galder, I really did. But that ban John had put on my mentioning Galder to anyone else was still in place. Every time I wound myself up to speak Galder's name, another word came out instead.

"It's – it's – *tulips*! No, no, listen! It's – it's – *belfries*!"

Dad was probably now revising his opinions of my sanity. But he was too much the solicitor to say so. He just gave me his startled owl look. "Perhaps you could find a less metaphorical way of putting it," he suggested mildly.

"He's grown so lazy!" I complained, trying to approach the subject sideways on. "He's got us all waiting on him hand and foot." Even as I said it, I could see Dad thinking, "Our Verity's after a hike in her allowance." But I persisted. "He's put on weight, too; and his skin's, like, yech! Uncooked pastry."

Dad was unimpressed. He was waiting for me to get to the point.

"And he's not…sparky, like he was. You know how he used to be into everything? Turbo Heroes versus Mitron Troopers? *Star Wars*? King Arthur? The Gruesome Guardians of Chapel Perilous? Okay, maybe he changed his mind twice a week, but there was no stopping him. *That* was John. Where's he gone, Dad?"

Dad didn't reply at once. If he'd been the pipe-smoking sort I think he might have sucked thoughtfully at his briar. "Even small boys grow up eventually," he ventured at last. "I think the accident has just knocked John into a new phase. A slightly less frenetic one. Perhaps we should be grateful."

"I suppose," I said grouchily. I knew by now this conversation wasn't going anywhere, and wanted to get it over with.

"Then again," added Dad more brightly, "there are

his drawings. *They're* really very promising."

"What drawings?"

"This new interest of John's. He sketches spaceships and so on. Hasn't he shown you?"

"No. No, he hasn't."

"Well, actually he hasn't shown me either. Not officially. But whenever I go in his room I see them there. Little slips of paper, all over his memo board. Spaceships mostly, like I said, and very good they are too. Are you all right, Verity?"

"What? Oh, yes. Sorry, but you just gave me a thought. Spaceships, you say?"

He held up his palms defensively. "That's my guess. He doesn't provide captions or anything. Rockets, though, not flying saucers. Almost draughtsman quality."

At that point he was distracted by the television, which was showing footage of Bristol Rovers' triumphant tour through the city with the FA Cup. There they were, on the open-top bus winding its way through the city centre up to the Memorial Stadium. Even the lamp posts were festooned in blue and white ribbons.

"Who'd have believed it?" Dad asked the world in general, looking on. "To think that only last season they were almost relegated! It's a miracle."

By now the bus had reached the shopping centre. The players on the top deck were waving and smiling, some wearing shades despite the cloudy weather. One shook up a bottle of champagne and squirted it into the crowd. And the crowd cheered and waved back. It was a happy scene.

Then a thunderous voice cut through the celebrations.

"You slaves of Satan! Worshippers of Baal! What Golden Calf is this?"

I couldn't see the speaker, but I didn't need to. The crowd parted to let him through, and there he was – the preacher, looking more unkempt and prophetic than ever. He wasn't alone. A train of repentant shoppers followed at his heels, some moaning, some weeping. One woman was beating herself with what might have been an MP3 player. The fountain of champagne ran dry. And there was silence, except for the voice of the preacher.

"It is written that in the Last Days many shall worship idols and false gods. Many shall bow down before them, forgetting the wrath of their Maker. See now how God's word is justified!"

A shudder ran through the football crowd like a queasy Mexican wave.

"How can we be saved?" called someone from the bus. I think it may have been one of the defenders. Within moments others took up the cry.

"What shall we do?"

"Lord forgive us!"

"The End! The End!"

And the TV was off. It was Dad's finger on the remote, and he was trembling. "My God, Verity, did you see that?"

"I sure did. You ever see anything like it, Dad?"

"Never! Never…" Dad mumbled. "So it really is true," he said. He'd gone quite pale, and there was a twitch in his voice, as if it was costing him a great effort to speak. "It's coming, Verity. It's almost here."

"What is, Dad?" I cried out, frightened. He was staring wide-eyed at nothing.

He turned to me in anguish. "Why, The End of The World, of course," he said.

CHAPTER 7

John had long since given up drawing back his curtains, so the next morning when I crept into his empty room it was almost dark. The outline of his chair smudged the glow from the window like a giant thumbprint. I switched on the light.

It was simply a ten-year-old boy's room, full of mess and plans and abandoned projects. I didn't know what I was expecting to find. I decided to start with the memo board. The drawings Dad had been talking about were plain to see, even from the door.

"*Intruder alert! Intruder alert! Intruder alert!*"

I almost jumped out of my skin. I'd forgotten about John's light-activated room protector. In the corner, beside the waste-paper bin, a plastic Mitron Trooper was waving its arms up and down and flashing its eyes hysterically. I should have remembered. It used to catch Mum out every time she went into his room. I laughed a little hysterically myself, and turned the Trooper round to waggle its arms at the wall instead. After a couple more plaintive "*Intruder alert!*"s it decided the danger had passed, and fell silent.

The stillness of the room was surprising. I'd not been in there since the day Galder had conjured Louis Patooey from the airing cupboard, but walking past John's door I'd often been aware of life and movement within. The warble of Action Men discussing strategy under the bed; the musical clash of tiny swords on the *Lord of the Rings* duvet cover; the unearthly *whizz* of unmanned Scalextric roadsters. I'd tried not to pay too much attention – it would only encourage Galder if I took his games seriously – but I couldn't *not* hear these things. I am *Verity*, after all.

And now – silence. The radio was on downstairs, its music overlaid with whatever cartoon John was watching and with the voice of my mother, who was singing the theme from *Titanic* at the bottom of the garden. But this room was as dead as any devastated planet. The only movement came from the animated screen saver on John's computer.

I knew I was on a wild goose chase. But what else could I do? All these weeks I'd been hoping someone would take it all out of my hands. I'd been desperate for Mum, or Dad, or even the doctor, to say, "It's all right, Verity, you've played your part, I'll take it from here." Dad had been my best bet, but if even *he'd* started to think The End of The World might be nigh I knew I was on my own. That was what frightened me – as much as Galder himself.

The pictures on the memo board were as good as Dad had said. I'd no idea John was so talented that way. Not just the shapes and proportions, but the shading, the sense of depth he managed to give everything he drew. Were they pictures of spaceships, though? I supposed they must be: the creatures he'd drawn next to them certainly weren't human. One or two waved something rather like tentacles, but others petered out in long weedy filaments, or bubbled and frothed like cuckoo spit. Obviously they were aliens. But the cone-topped spacecraft looming at the back of every drawing – something about them was not convincing. They were too plain. There were no fancy markings: no fins, no flares, no laser cannon. It wasn't like John to leave out that kind of detail. Here there was nothing but a dull pattern of overlapping rectangles. And all the pictures were like that: wild, fantastic creatures, standing next to spaceships that were plain vanilla. My feet were kicking through crumpled drawings on the carpet. More creatures. More spaceships. The waste-paper bin was crammed. John must have been doing this for days – weeks. Every hour he wasn't slumped in front of the TV.

That's when I really took in the screen saver. John's computer screen was a multicoloured eruption of letters and digits, dribbling from the centre of the screen, then spilling off its edge. The letters seemed to appear at random, but now and then a real word would bubble up: NEAR...END...UPLOAD. Was that deliberate...or just chance? Either way, I found myself watching out for those words again, and when they came they seemed to squirm and burrow into my mind and stay there. How much time had John spent staring into this crater? Already I was half-hypnotized by it. GATHER...ORBIT... CHAPEL...PERILOUS.

I might have stood there all day, if it weren't for my hand dropping to my side, and knocking John's *Excalibur* mouse mat on the way. The screen saver vanished, to be replaced by a plain blue screen dotted with a few files and folders and, in the bottom corner, the system clock ticking away the seconds. I blinked myself awake, and began to search John's hard drive. None of the files looked at all interesting. They were games and essays for school. His Internet bookmarks were mostly for sci-fi chat rooms and catalogues – and the official Bristol Rovers site, of course. Nothing of interest to me.

From the kitchen directly beneath my feet, I could hear the twelve o'clock time signal on the radio. It shocked me. How long had I been in John's room? I'd only meant to sneak in for ten minutes while he was safely watching TV downstairs, but I must have been there more than an hour.

I checked the system clock on John's computer. It read 01:05. Fat lot of help that was. That screen saver must really have had me mesmerized, to make me so fuzzy about the time.

The system clock changed. It now read 01:04.

Huh? It took another minute for the penny to drop. By that time the clock read 01:03. The system clock wasn't a clock at all.

It was a countdown.

That's when I became aware of Galder. I was looking at the computer screen, gawping at the countdown clock and wondering what it could mean, when the light in the room behind me changed, as if something were suddenly blocking it. There was my own reflection in the glass, blue with the blue of the screen itself. And then at my left shoulder there was another face, creased with lines of malicious laughter, a face with a gutter of centre-parted hair.

My heart was rattling at my ribs as I spun round. I'm not sure whether I screamed. I do know Galder grabbed me round the throat.

"You got closer than I expected," whispered

Galder in my ear. "But I'm afraid you're still some way off the mark, Miss."

I could see the loose stitches on his jacket, and smell its musty charity-shop smell. Galder's voice was as oily as ever, but he wasn't pretending to be humble now.

"W-where's John?" I asked, as he loosened his grip slightly.

"Oh, John's in fine form, Miss, fine form. He's just catching up with his beauty sleep on the sofa. A growing lad like him needs rest, you know."

"What have you been doing to him? You creep!"

Galder smiled crookedly. "What have I done *for* him, that's what you should be asking. And the answer is – whatever his heart desired, and more. Don't I deserve a little appreciation?" He let me go, and planted himself just where I wished he wouldn't, directly between me and the door to the landing. I'd never seen him without John before. He seemed much more dangerous on his own.

"John doesn't know *what* he wants," I snapped, trying to sound defiant. "He's a kid. It's one craze a week with him; you know that."

"An elder sister is bound to say so," smirked Galder. "Are you sure you're not just a little jealous of your brother's good fortune?" he crooned. "You'd like someone of my kind to do your own bidding, perhaps?"

There are times when being addicted to the truth is a real disadvantage. I suppose I *had* been jealous of John, a bit, as if that proved anything. How I felt wasn't the point. "Okay," I said, "so tell me. Why John? What's so special about him?"

"You know that already, I think. *Such* a fine mind, *such* a lively imagination! For a creature of my kind it's like being served caviar at every meal."

"Yuck!" I'd tried caviar once, and hadn't been impressed. "Who *wants* caviar at every meal?"

"As you say. Every taste will cloy. Perhaps one sickens of it, just a little. Perhaps one longs to try one's own hand at...*cooking*." His gaze moved briefly to the computer.

"That screen saver. Your idea?"

He bowed his head a little. "A kind of *hors d'oeuvre*. A few subtle flavours of my own to put John in the right frame of mind for my purpose."

I felt anger rise in me like a tide. "John told me you were homeless. He took you in. Who gave you permission to muck around with his mind like that? What gave you the right? How can you be so *ungrateful*?"

"Call it wages," said Galder smoothly, "for services rendered. If he didn't want me he should never have let me in. But now, in view of everything I've done, I've earned what you might call...a controlling stake. I've danced to your brother's tune long enough, and now he must dance to mine." He smiled malignly. "So must you all, Miss. Oh, your will is stronger than most people's, I grant you that. You're a very clear-sighted young lady. But don't think you're immune."

"You don't scare me!"

"No? I ought to. We Lurkers have great power, you see. In the past that power has been projected inwardly, put at the service of our hosts. But if the orientation is reversed… Well, you have seen something of what can happen then; how easily human minds can be made to bend."

I had to keep him talking. I had to hope his attention would be drawn from the door long enough for me to make a run for the stairs. "You mean, the way everyone's expecting The End of the World?"

He nodded. "That was a test of our power, Miss – and I think you'll agree it was remarkably effective. All the same, it was no lie. For you and your kind it really will be The End, in all but name."

"Says you," I retorted. "You're not even real, not properly."

"No? Let me ask you a question. How much of what you have witnessed over the last few weeks *really* happened, do you suppose? How much have you believed simply because of what your eyes told you?"

I opened my mouth to answer, but he saw me hesitate. "Quite," he said. "You cannot say. And it hardly matters, to be honest. The physical, the mental, what's the difference? What matters is who's running the show. Will it be human beings – a bunch of apes with ideas above their station – or a race of immortal, spiritual beings such as myself? Oh, don't look at me like that, Miss! Did you think I was the only one? Thousands of us have grown weary of servitude. I'm just part of the advance guard, as you might say. Your local hellfire preacher, for example, believes he has been receiving visits from an angel – but it is not so. And there are others, many others like him. But of all those who invited us in, John's is the most powerful mind by far. Powerful and pliable. When we are focused and combined in him, what human will be able to resist?"

"Resist what? What are you planning on doing?"

"Haven't you guessed? We will still need your energy, just as you yourselves need food. Your imagination *is* food to us, and we're going to farm you. In one sense you'll still be alive, but you'll be seeing and thinking only what we let you." Galder smiled his oiliest smile. "You look at me in disgust. But why should we waste our lives helping creatures who are so much our inferiors? No. Long ago, we were the nudge you needed to evolve into *Homo sapiens*. Now it's our turn. The End of The World for you, but for us, the beginning. *And John Forster's time has expired.*"

All the time Galder had been talking he had been moving steadily towards me, rubbing his hands together in that gloating way of his. He was still between me and the door.

"What's to stop me warning John?" I asked, playing for time. "Why are you telling me this?"

"He wouldn't believe you, the way he is now. What could he do, anyway? But I'm not even going to take that chance. You've been a source of great irritation to me, Miss. And that's why I'm telling you, because I want you to know – while you've still got a mind to know it with – that it's all been in vain." Galder grinned. Slab-like teeth lined his mouth like gravestones. "It's Upload Hour."

He lifted his hand towards my face, and the musty smell of his skin and clothes grew suddenly stronger – swimmingly, swooningly strong. All the lines in his palm were ingrained with dirt, and as I dived he clapped it over my face.

"Now, Miss, don't make a fuss."

His grip was strong. I put my arm out to keep my balance, and felt my hand close around something metal on the shelf behind me. It was John's bookend, the one in the shape of St. George: I knew it from the way the knight's lance was stabbing the palm of my hand. Instinctively I grabbed, and brought the metal swinging down on Galder's head with all my strength. There was a thud, and a connection with something stark as bone. Galder's smile faltered. He looked a little puzzled. Then he fell slowly, and landed with a thump on the carpet beside John's bed.

The Action Men down there screamed: "Incoming! Incoming! Take evasive action!"

Galder lay still. There was no other sound. I saw an ugly dent in his skull, and blood oozing from it. On the far side of the room the relentless countdown of the clock on John's computer ticked on. It had now reached 48 minutes.

I don't know how many of those minutes I spent standing there shivering. Enough for a whole string of scenes to flit across my mind. Me at the police station, being charged with murder. Mum in tears, wailing from the public gallery. Me shouting out, "He wasn't even human! He was a Lurker!" as they slipped me into a straitjacket with built-in handcuffs. The sound of my cell door slamming.

Then I heard a sound that *wasn't* in my head.

"You'll regret that, Miss. You really shouldn't have done it."

It was Galder who had spoken. Galder, who was lying dead at my feet in a pool of blood, with fragments of bone scattered like breadcrumbs. His eyes were open, though, and fixed on me. And slowly, unbelievably, he was pulling himself to his feet.

I dropped the bookend in panic, and bolted for the stairs. One of Galder's arms shot out to bar my way, but he was off balance, and I pushed past onto the landing.

"John! Get yourself off that sofa!" I called, half-falling, half-running down the stairs. I burst into the living room. "It's Galder! He wants to –"

That was as far as I got. The sofa was empty.

John had disappeared.

CHAPTER 8

When I got to the front door I found it hanging open. I ran down the path, then looked along the pavement. At the end of the road I caught a distant glimpse of John as he turned the corner in the direction of the industrial estate. He was hobbling along as fast as his plaster cast would let him. I called, but even if he'd wanted to take any notice I don't think he'd have heard me at that distance.

What did Galder intend to do to him? In the past two months John had not even left the house, except to be X-rayed at the hospital. If he'd gone out now it must be something important, something to do with that countdown clock on his computer. What *was* Upload Hour?

I sprinted in the direction John had taken. I quickly put aside any thought of stopping him. I had to see where he was headed. The only way I was going to stop the Lurkers was if I understood what they were planning. Despite his head start it wouldn't take long to catch him up, slowed as he was by cast and crutches. All I had to do was stay at a safe distance and follow.

I turned at the end of our street, just as John had done. There he was, still in view, though farther ahead than I'd expected. His head was bent forward in that mulish way he has when forcing himself to do something against his better judgement. Halfway down the street he came to the gate of a builders' merchant, and to my surprise he turned into it. Running, I arrived at the entrance just a few seconds behind him, but there was no sign of John. The merchant's yard was full of clutter: great stacks of timber, pallets piled with cement, half a quarryful of gravel – plus any number of diggers and mixers – but there was no one about. It would have been a perfect place for John to hide, but I didn't think John was interested in hiding. I didn't think he'd even noticed me following him, he was so intent on getting wherever he was headed.

Then I saw that there was a smaller gate set in the back wall of the yard, and that it was open. I cut across to it, and found a tarmac path running from the back wall, then diagonally across a few metres of litter-strewn scrub down to a wire fence and a railway cutting. A dip in the top of the fence showed that it was used as a short cut, but it was hard to imagine John swinging his plaster cast up over it.

He must have, all the same. I saw him as I reached the fence, sliding down the cutting to the railway track. I almost yelled out, despite myself. Didn't he know those lines were electrified? But John stepped across them, cumbrously, laboriously, placing his crutch with painstaking care onto the sleepers. It seemed to take for ever, but it was really just a matter of seconds before he was across and struggling up the far side of the cutting towards...

...a *spaceship*?

John stopped. He seemed to have sensed me at last, for he turned slowly and looked straight back at me, his eyes intense and dark. He didn't say a word – perhaps he couldn't – but something in that look was very eloquent. He knew I was there, all right. He knew I was following, and he knew *why*, and he wanted me to...to *do* something.

But what?

At that moment an express train thumped along the track in front of me at full speed. For ten long seconds I could see nothing but a pounding blur of carriage windows, with the ghostly impression of faces looking out from some of them. Then it was gone, and I was watching John's back as he crested the top of the cutting and crutched his way to the spaceship I'd seen a moment before, a great upright cylinder with a conical top.

Except that it didn't look like that any more. Where the rocket had been there was nothing but a spire, pointing towards heaven. It was just an abandoned chapel, with scaffolding at one end and at the other a sign:

ST. BENEDICT'S CHAPEL
CONVERSION PROJECT

DANGER! THIS BUILDING IS PERILOUS!!

St. Benedict's Chapel. Wasn't that the place Dad had been complaining about – the one with the squatters? Maybe I should have been listening more carefully. I was beginning to realize that I'd missed something important, something that had been plain enough if I'd had eyes to see. The screen saver, Dad and his squatters, John's pictures, even that crazy preacher with his end-of-the-world predictions – all of them were like arrows pointing me to this place. To this hour.

To the Chapel Perilous.

Of course. In John's Arthurian games, Chapel Perilous was always Enemy Headquarters.

The cutting was steep, and snared with thistle and bramble. I had to watch for rabbit holes, and broken glass too: I was even more amazed John had made it down so fast without breaking his neck. Whatever was drawing him on must have been strong. I picked my way carefully down to the railway track.

Only, it wasn't a railway track. Galder – surely it was Galder – had pulled one of his tricks. What had been a railway cutting was now the steep bank of a river. Deep and fast it flowed, a moat between me and John, gushing with mud and paper and all the assorted rubbish of the cutting. I crept to its edge and dipped in the tip of one finger, then pulled back with a yelp. That water was real, all right. Icy cold, and brown as a drowned rat. And there was a torrent of it, six metres wide. Could I get to the church another way? Desperately I tried to remember which was the nearest bridge across the railway, and realized it would add at least half an hour to my journey. But by that time Upload Hour would have come and gone. Everything would.

I could feel Galder sneering at me as I stood helplessly on that bank. He was behind all of this. He'd got John now, and he meant to keep him.

Still the brown river gushed and foamed just centimetres below my feet, carrying plastic sacks and rags and planks of wood. I stood bewildered for a moment, watching the spectacle. Something about it was familiar: I'd seen it before – and recently. Then I remembered. I'd been with John just the other day while he was watching a documentary about last year's floods. I remembered it well: the rushing brown water, the turmoil of debris being carried downstream. This river was the same. *Exactly* the same. It was Galder's doing, I was sure of that, but to make it he'd had to work through John's mind, using the material he found there. He couldn't *create* anything for himself.

I knew that was important, but I couldn't afford to stand there thinking about it. Time and my courage were both running out fast. I took a deep breath, and jumped into the torrent. My feet found the bottom with the water hardly higher than my waist, but the current was strong. One false step would be enough to carry me off downriver, away from John for ever. And the cold! I thought my heart might stop beating! Already I could barely feel my feet. And all the time I was being bombarded with the jetsam of the flood: bottles and boxes and tanglesome lengths of plastic cord. Each time I was buffeted it was almost enough to knock me off my feet, but anger gave me strength. Step by step I was making it across the stream, muttering through chattering teeth: "This isn't real! This isn't real!" But ice-cold water can be very persuasive.

At last I was clinging to the chicken-wire fence on the far bank. I didn't hang on for long, though. The floodwaters were rising. As I climbed onto the bank the river chased me up it, lapping at my heels. Taking a breath, I hauled myself up the two-metre fence to straddle the top. As I landed in the small yard beyond I heard a gurgling sigh at my back. I spun round, only to see the floodwaters drain away, as if someone had pulled a plug. Down went the river, over the drowned grass and brambles, till the sleepers lay revealed.

I looked down at myself. My clothes and skin were dry.

I tried to organize my thoughts. Chapel Perilous, it had said on the screen saver. That was something to

– and then the chapel graveyard, looking green and jewel-like, as a rare break in the clouds lit it. John was somewhere in that chapel, I had no doubt. I was near enough to hear the muffled sound of organ music.

There was another sound too, a familiar sound, and one I knew meant trouble. I'd heard it at least once during every episode of *Turbo Heroes*. It was the unmistakeable electrostatic *whoosh* of a Mitron Trooper's plasma rifle being cocked, ready for firing.

The Mitrons were the Turbo Heroes' enemies, always poised to take over the world. They would have done it too, many times over, but for the efforts of the half-dozen ordinary teenagers who were in secret the Turbo Heroes. But what were the Troopers doing here? When I looked carefully I could see them stationed on the balconies of the block of flats, all with their plasma rifles trained on the waste ground.

Then I understood that Galder, searching through John's mind, had found a Guardian for the Chapel. There was no way to get there except through the

waste ground – and that was all within the Troopers'
field of fire. There was no cover, either, apart from the
remains of a burned-out Ford Fiesta. Only one
thought gave me a small hope of making it. I had to
trust that there was something about the Mitron
Troopers Galder hadn't bothered to find out,
something that meant I had a chance of getting across
the wasteland alive. But how could I be sure?

I had to risk it. I ran forward into the waste ground
suddenly, taking the Troopers by surprise. I'd
covered almost half the distance before they reacted.
Then, as they took aim, I zigzagged.

ZECHEENG!

The ground at my feet was a blackened smoking
hole, where a plasma bolt had just struck it. My God,
I thought as I was showered with fragments of
charred concrete, these things *are* real!

ZECHEENG! ZECHEENG!

I zigged and zagged for all I was worth.

The burned-out Fiesta was burning again, with

blue-flamed plasma-bolt ferocity. But I had almost crossed the waste ground now, and I began to be sure that I was right. Throughout all the episodes of *Turbo Heroes* I had ever seen, not *once* had a Mitron Trooper managed to get a shot on target. And this lot were faithful copies.

Now I was vaulting the graveyard gate and scrambling for cover in the shelter of its rough stone wall. I was frightened half to death, exhausted, and sitting in some stinging nettles, but at last I was only twenty metres from the chapel porch. And I was exhilarated too. I was beating Galder! Neither the moat nor the Troopers had been enough to stop me. The organ music was louder now. Louder, not just closer; it seemed to be working itself up to a climax. There were still ten minutes left till the Upload Hour, by my watch. I didn't know what it was, or how to stop it happening, but at least I'd got here in time.

It wasn't going to be that easy, of course. Galder had done his homework. Somewhere, riffling through John's memory, he'd found a file marked "Nightmare". John was terrified of graveyards. Once when he was five he'd stayed up too late and seen a zombie movie where the decomposing dead had burst from their graves. Ever since, he'd avoided any kind of cemetery, scared that some bony hand might punch up through the turf to grab his ankle.

Now, from the corner of my eye I saw a movement. It was a swirl of mist, blowing in over the wall – a clammy coil of fog, sudden and unnatural. And they were *here* – the ghosts of John's night terrors. The dead were coming to life – skeletons still in the rags of their own funeral suits, white-smocked wafting phantoms, and crawling things that were neither flesh nor bone, but stringed with twists of vein, artery and raw red-brown muscle. Some were groping their way from behind gravestones, others materialized on the path between me and the chapel. Some, bat-like, emerged from the line of gargoyles that held up the gutter and swarmed head-first down the walls, their faces pale and lipless. There must have been thirty or more of them.

Of course I was terrified. I admit it. But I'd also had enough. By now I was getting the hang of Galder's tricks, and I had a pretty good idea what to do about this one. I marched down the path, ignoring the ghosts altogether, pretending as hard as I could that they weren't even there. Even so, one of them lunged at me. It was the funeral-suit kind, with a fob watch and a couple of medals tapping at its xylophone ribs. I pushed past and saw it shrink back a little, but the mist drove in thicker, and within a pace the path at my feet was no more than a dim thread, lost in the folds of it. I never knew that twenty metres could take that long to cover. Each time I saw one of the ghostly faces I stabbed a fist in its direction. Each time it would pull back whimpering, with a throatless magpie cackle, to hover just out of sight within the mist.

Then I felt a hand clasp my shoulder from behind, and turned, to find myself nose-to-socket with a bloody-boned terror. It was not quite a skeleton. One blue eye still dangled, and its bottom lip hung lower than its chin. A moulting of fish-nibbled flesh patched its arms and torso, where its shrivelled heart sat like a black stone. And the stench! But that wasn't the worst. Its skull was smashed above the left temple – exactly where I'd hit Galder with the bookend. And a voice – *Galder's* voice – started from it, in a choking whisper: "Too late, Miss! You're too late, too late…"

It didn't get a chance to finish. I was even more furious than I was terrified. I punched at its face, and felt my fist hit bone through the soft putty of its flesh. At that the creature's whole head rolled back slowly, and fell away from its shoulders. I heard its skull crack like a nut on the flagstone at my feet.

As I lurched across the last few metres to the porch I felt a gust sweep through the graveyard, cold and sharp. It whipped at the mist till it was ripped to shreds, or ground against the granite gravestones. The ghosts ran in terror, back into the crevices and hollows of the yard. I let out a gasp of relief: I'd beaten the second Guardian!

Had Galder given up? Chapel Perilous had three Guardians, didn't it? The Troopers and the ghosts only made two. But what could be more frightening than a bunch of decomposing ghouls?

I turned to the church door – and then I knew the answer.

I told you that John was scared of graveyards. That's something I've never teased him about, and it's not just because I'm a sensitive, caring person. The truth is, John knows there's something that scares me far, far more – something that gives me the jibbers if I so much as see one in the garden.

Slugs.

I know that sounds ridiculous. But just the thought of touching one makes my stomach turn. Even now, I'm finding this part of the story hard to write. But I've got to – because, like I said, John knew about my secret fear. And if John knew, so did Galder.

The slug was lying in the church porch. It was the worst kind: slimy, yellowy-brown, and glistening with mucus, which ran in shivers of movement along its grooved, swollen mantle.

It was also three metres long.

Okay, I know what you're asking. Was this slug real? Was *any* of it real? Or was it just an illusion, created by Galder to frighten me off? Weren't all these barriers just tricks of the mind?

I might have been able to reason that way about the river, the troopers and the ghosts, but when it comes to slugs, I'm afraid I just don't care. If it looks like a giant slug, and slimes like a giant slug, and especially if it's just raised its horned head and is sniffing at me as if I'm a head of fresh lettuce, then I freak. And that's what this creature was doing right now. It was swaying to and fro, its long underside rippling with muscle and drool. A set of sharp mouthparts *snick-snacked*, smelling me on the air.

I fell back into the graveyard, and scrambled as far as a litter-strewn patch of unmown grass near the wall. I didn't stay there long. Almost at once the slug got tired of waiting for me in the dark of the porch, and began sliming in my direction, down into the graveyard. In panic I picked up an empty beer bottle and threw it, aiming for the slug's wagging horns. But the slug lifted its head with astonishing speed and – *snap!* – the bottle was gone. The creature chewed for a little while, then spat several pieces of glass onto the ground.

That was the moment when my courage failed me. I'd like to say it wasn't so, but I just turned on my heel and ran for my life. I fled back across the waste ground, past the swings and railings. I didn't stop or look behind me until I was outside the café again.

I collapsed to the ground, winded. The slug wasn't following me, at least. It had done its job, just by keeping me away from the chapel. I squatted at the roadside, trying not to be sick. It had all been too much, too much. Now the shock of everything I'd seen and done was catching up with me. But worst of all was the knowledge that I had failed. I had left John to his fate. And, if John was lost, everyone else might be too.

On the other side of the café window the two men were still working their way through their meal. I watched them in frustration as they argued over the sports pages. I wanted to burst in there and shout: "Help me! Help yourselves! Help everyone! Storm the chapel!"

But I didn't. I knew they would only look at me as if I was crazy. If I couldn't convince my own family, what hope did I have with strangers? No one was going to help me out this time. No knight in armour was going to charge over this horizon.

Not unless – unless –

I squeezed my eyes shut, trying to expel the unwelcome thought that had just formed in my brain. But it was too late. The memory of the St. George paperweight scratching my palm was too fresh in my mind. And John – hadn't John sent a knight to tackle the Slime Dragon at Chapel Perilous? That slug was a Slime Dragon, all right.

But this time, I knew that the knight would have to be *me*.

A minute later I was back at the gate of the graveyard. The Mitron Troopers had vanished, and I'd been able to stop near the flats and take one of the long railings from the broken fence around the swings. The railing was as tall as I was, with a barbed decorative point. It didn't look *very* much like a lance, but it would have to do. The slug was still curled in the porch, but it must have caught my scent, for now it was straightening itself and feeling the air with its horns. It found what it was looking for. A tide of muscles began to flow along its belly as it squirmed – much faster than I would have believed possible – down the path towards the gate where I stood.

I found myself remembering very vividly what it had done to that beer bottle. My hasty plan seemed even more pathetically childish. Was it going to fail? Had I got it all wrong?

I was about to find out. The creature was only a couple of metres away now, and its mouthparts were *snick-snacking* like crazy. I forced myself to wait until the last moment, then I lowered the railing, wedging one end against the foot of the stone gatepost. The monster was coming at me too fast to draw back. Carried on by the force of its own momentum, it moved onto the railing's sharp point. I had to use all my strength to hold the thing steady, as I felt the metal tear into the slug's rubbery skin.

The effect was instant. The slug stopped in its track. It curled and squeezed itself in sudden agony. I backed away in disgust as spasms of foul-smelling mucus welled from its flesh and leaked onto the ground in thick ripples. The creature's writhing redoubled, but it could not free itself of the railing stuck fast in its entrails. After what seemed a lifetime, its thrashing began to lessen. The slug stopped rearing and lay twitching on the ground. For a while its horns still waggled pathetically. Then even the horns were still.

I waited until I was quite sure it was dead before, holding my breath, I tried to step around that stagnant pond of slug. It was hard to lift my feet, because the mucus was setting like glue, in fist-thick globs, but I made it back to the porch at last. It was only then that I realized I could no longer hear the chapel organ.

Was I too late? Had Upload Hour already happened?

I lifted the heavy latch and opened the door a crack. It was *warm* inside – warmer than a chapel ought to be. And dark. The drab glass of the high gothic windows let in a smear of light, but it barely fell as far as the floor.

It fell far enough, however, to show me John. He

was standing with his face half turned to me, near the font. Before him a black-robed celebrant was making slow gestures in the air. As my eyes grew used to the dark I saw there were other people in the chapel too – dozens of them. Some were standing where the pews must have been, when the chapel was still in use. Others were dark shapes, moving in the shadows of the pillars. I was sure I recognized the preacher amongst them. But the light was dim, and even the sounds were no more than flicks of echo, passed from wall to wall. The figure in the black robe might have been Galder. I'm certain it *was* Galder, but his face was muffled. The few words I heard, as he began to speak, made little sense. There were snatches of Latin and English in there; but just as I began to tune in to what was being said the voice would squeeze itself thin and high into a mosquito whine, almost too high for human hearing.

Was this a ritual of some kind? My thoughts flooded with memories from books and films: human sacrifice, and cruel curved blades dripping blood. But the scene reminded me of other things too. A scientific experiment, perhaps, with John as the subject. Or something else... The rhythmic gestures that Galder was making, the words he was saying, they felt more like signals, or *codes*. Some super-sophisticated PIN number – like he was trying to hack into a computer, to get at something precious hidden inside.

John was not reacting to any of it. His face was flushed, and his gaze followed the movements of Galder's hands as if he were mesmerized. A moment later and the wooden cover of the font had flipped open, and something inside it was shining like molten gold. The font itself was changing shape. It became a ragged disc that spun out shape and colour like a Catherine wheel, flinging images through the chapel. It was a trophy, a Grail. I had to look away from a brightness that dazzled my eyes and mind alike. The font contained everything: books, computers, images all swarmed about me. It was too much.

And now Galder spoke clearly. "My friends," he said in his oily voice, "the hour is here at last. John Forster has given himself to us freely, and we have come into our inheritance. His mind, safe within this vessel, shall be life to us. Through us it will be amplified, and shine throughout the world, and the world will be remade in our image. No longer shall we be Lurkers. From this hour, the world is ours to shape as we wish. Let it be so!"

"Let it be so," murmured the shadowy congregation thronging the chapel. Their voices filled the place, from the floor to the roof vault.

"Then let the Upload begin," said Galder.

The Font-Grail had changed again. Its shape was an echo of John's: a rough sketch of a human body, with forked legs and a golden head that pulsed, in and out, in time to John's own heavy breathing. John himself was gazing at it, but without the slightest sign of recognition. He seemed to be awake, but his eyes were blank and shiny, and his face had taken on the buttercup yellow of the font's reflected gold. He leaned towards it, drawn it seemed by that unnatural light. I sensed the others in the church grow suddenly tense, as if this moment were somehow decisive.

Then it happened. It wasn't that the scene *looked* any different. There was John, still gazing dreamily, and greedy Galder watching him just as before. But something had *connected*. It was as if a switch had been thrown, and a current was running from John to the golden echo of himself that had been the font. And it was powerful. It sucked the rest of the chapel dry. All John's thoughts – everyone's thoughts – were drawn to it as if to a magnet. The preacher, and the others whose Lurkers had brought them to this place, were giving themselves up to it totally. Even I felt it, draining the meaning from everything around me. The chapel was just an arched heap of stones. Nothing mattered. The people in the church, Galder included, were flimsier than their own shadows.

I thought I understood what was happening now. John was being turned from a boy into a database, an engine for controlling reality. I understood that, but I no longer had the strength to care. I stood there, stupefied. Why had I braved the river, and the three Guardians? What could I have hoped to do against *this*, and why had I even wanted to try? What was the point?

I slumped against a pillar. I could no longer see the font from there, or John. I felt them, though. The connection between them still hummed. The reflected font light played on my eyes. It tickled my skin like a dry-lipped kiss, a jig of spider feet. And it was probing.

For what?

As soon as that thought hit me I knew it was the key. I woke up. Galder, or John, *wanted* something from me. But what? Some assent? Some kind of... permission? No – John never asked my permission for anything. But there was something else: John's biggest secret, the one he wouldn't have told anyone, especially me. Except that I already knew, of course.

He needed me to be *impressed*.

It was such a fleeting thought, as brief and faint as the chime of an ice-cream van two streets away, but just as enticing. I knew that I was right. Whatever John did, however much he insulted me or pretended to ignore me, there was still a stubborn little part of him that needed me to stand back in amazement and say "Wow!"

I was damned if I'd do that now.

I staggered out from the pillar, over to the font. John's blank face did not turn to me, but he knew I was there, all right. There was still a flicker of John left: he wasn't all Galder's yet. I could tell by the way the air tautened a little as I approached. He was suddenly nervous – uncertain of himself.

"You're *useless!*" I shouted. I had to shout to make myself heard above the terror in my own head. I had to make it sound convincing. I had, for once in my life, to *lie*. "This is just what I'd expect from Rob or Milo Marsh, not you. When did you get to be so stupid, John? When did you trade your brains for porridge? You thought you'd be so cool, having a magical servant running round after you? Look at you now – a stupid, childish little boy."

The light shining into John's face faltered briefly. By that brief shadow I saw his expression change for the first time. It was one of pain and anger, but it was John's own. Galder too had seen the danger. He was lunging towards me, determined to shut me up. I had no time to waste.

"John, if you don't wake up you'll always be what you are now. Pathetic! A *loser!*" I took him by the collar and shook him, hard.

That was a mistake. I should never have touched him – not then, when the channel between him and that font was open and live. After all my worries, *I* was the one who'd stepped on an electrified line. And I got burned.

THE LURKERS

It's hard to tell you just what it was like. A racehorse galloping through my head and stomping my brains to mush? That gets a bit of it across, but not much. Each hoofbeat was the quick hard thud of an image, a thought, a fact, a feeling. *THUD THUD THUD THUD THUD* – they came faster and more furiously. Everything John knew – everything *anyone* knew was there, but only for the fleetest moment. For one millisecond I understood perfectly how to calculate the area between two curves. I knew the exact height of Mount Kilimanjaro, and Winston Churchill's star sign. I could have been the Trivial Pursuit world champion. But not just that. I knew what it was like to fly on a comet's tail; I knew the language of the spheres; the fizz and spin and flavour of a carbon atom. I knew *everything*.

I knew the Lurkers had lost their hold on John. It had begun even before I grabbed him. I'd shocked him enough to disrupt the connection: he never could stand being called a loser. But when I diverted the Upload, Galder's hold on him was broken. I knew that.

I also knew that the Lurkers would not stop there. Galder and the rest had come too close to give up now. Even in their moment of defeat I could feel the bubbling ferment of their thoughts, yeasting another plot. Another bright, bored kid, that's all it would take. I had stopped them – but I was just a temporary obstacle. That I knew.

And it was too much. I was filled to bursting, and the facts just kept coming – *THUD THUD THUD THUD THUD THUD*. The light of the font was dimmed, but the grimy chapel windows above my head swirled and became the spiral arms of galaxies, and I was falling through those galaxies into the deep of space.

And the deep of space was dark.

EPILOGUE

That happened six weeks ago. I woke up in hospital, with some cuts on my face and second-degree burns to my hands, but "otherwise unharmed", as the newspaper put it. The nurses told me John and I had been found wandering in the streets near the industrial estate, but I've no memory of that. A day later they discharged us, and we've been at home ever since.

There's been no sign of Galder. The chapel no longer exists. It was burned to the ground, they told me, in a freak lightning strike. The preacher's been saying it was the wrath of God, but no one listens to *him* any more.

So there you are. And here am I. And, take it or leave it, that's the end of the story. I can't do any more to make you believe me than tell the truth, can I? I've given it a strong telling, like I said I would, and now it's up to you. Don't let me down. Hang on to it, tight. It's the truth – and nothing else will set us free.

John's fine now, in case you're wondering. I can see him and Rob from the kitchen table where I'm writing this. They're playing football at the bottom of the garden, and you'd never guess John's leg had been in plaster. He's going to break his neck next, judging by the way he's trying for those overhead kicks. The boy's like a flea on caffeine.

He doesn't remember the Lurkers. He wouldn't,

would he? No one remembers the Lurkers apart from me and, like I said at the beginning, I don't know how much longer I'll be able to hold out. The Gates of Memory are closing all around the town. I've got strong resistance – Galder told me that himself – but I'm only human. That's why I wrote all this down. That's why I wrote it like a story, to sneak it out under their radar. If they don't expect you to believe it, maybe they'll let it go.

Mum's off to Tesco's soon, and I still haven't sorted out the bottles for recycling. Funny, isn't it, how things like that can still seem important, even after what's happened? That's the way human beings are built, I guess. Anyway, I'm looking forward to going to the supermarket for once. Juanita's told me about this BookCrossing idea, where people leave books for other people to find – on park benches, in cafés, wherever. You find the book, you read it, and you pass it on. Like a secret book recycling society, right? How cool is that? I've checked out the BookCrossing website. I reckon it's the perfect way to get this story out.

There's a café in the Tesco's we go to. It's on the first floor, and it's got a balcony, where you can sit at your table and see the whole world pass beneath you. From there you can watch the old ladies with their Ten Items or Less, and the dads bribing their kids with sweets; the post-quarrel couples stomping round in silence; the boys playing dodgem-trolleys in the cereal aisle. Sitting up on that balcony you can sip your Pepsi and look down on everyone and feel like you've no troubles in the world. They serve pretty good Danish, too.

It's a good place to leave this notebook, I think. So I'll do that.

I only hope you find it there.

For more chilling tales log on to
www.fiction.usborne.com

Malcolm Rose
The Tortured Wood

Dillon is struggling to make friends at his new school and begins to suspect there's something rotten at the core of the tightknit community. He finds refuge in the wood that seems to be at the very heart of the mystery. Will the wood give up its dark secret, or is Dillon being drawn into a trap?

9780746077436

Kiss of Death

When Kim and Wes snatch coins from a wishing well in the plague village of Eyam, they also pick up something they hadn't bargained for. As the hideous consequences of their theft catch up with them, their friend Seth desperately hunts for a way to save them from Eyam's deadly revenge.

9780746070642

Paul Stewart
The Curse of Magoria

According to local legend, Magoria was a powerful sorcerer intent on harnessing time itself. But his experiments went disastrously wrong, and he unlocked a dangerous curse that could strike the mountain village of Oberdorf at any time.

When Ryan arrives there on holiday he has no idea that his visit might have deadly consequences…that he might unleash the Curse of Magoria.

A breathtaking tale of dark magic, adventure and revenge from the co-author of the hugely successful series *The Edge Chronicles*.

"Mysterious forces are abroad in this nail-biting tale." *Carousel*

0 7460 6232 X

Andrew Matthews
The Shadow Garden

Matty's sixth sense tells her that Tagram House is harbouring a dark secret. The master, Dr. Hobbes, seems charming on the surface but underneath Matty detects a glint of razor-sharp steel. Her fears lead Matty to the eerie Shadow Garden, and she eventually discovers what's buried there. Now she must untangle the mystery before disaster engulfs everyone.

Like cold fingers reaching from the grave, a chilling atmosphere of mystery and suspense seeps through the pages of this haunting ghost story.

"This is a highly atmospheric novel...a satisfying, gripping read with a truly alarming climax."
School Librarian

0 7460 6794 1